Ju
F
Sa 1   Sachs, Marilyn.
            What my sister
        remembered.

Temple Israel Library
Minneapolis, Minn.

———

Please sign your full name on the above
card.

Return books promptly to the Library or
Temple Office.

Fines will be charged for overdue books
or for damage or loss of same.

WHAT MY SISTER REMEMBERED

Also by Marilyn Sachs

WHAT MY SISTER REMEMBERED

MARILYN SACHS

▼▼▼▼▼▼▼

DUTTON CHILDREN'S BOOKS
NEW YORK

Library of Congress Cataloging-in-Publication Data
Sachs, Marilyn.
    What my sister remembered / by Marilyn Sachs.—1st ed.
       p.   cm.
    Summary: While visiting her younger sister Molly, Beth
confronts painful memories of the sudden death of her parents
and the subsequent adoption of the sisters by different families.
    ISBN 0-525-44953-1
    [1. Sisters—Fiction. 2. Family problems—Fiction. 3. Emotional
problems—Fiction. 4. Adoption—Fiction.] I. Title.
PZ7.S1187Wh 1992   √91-32263
[Fic]—dc20   CIP
                            AC

Published in the United States by Dutton Children's Books,
a division of Penguin Books USA Inc.
375 Hudson Street, New York, New York 10014

Editor: Ann Durell   Designer: Joseph Rutt

Printed in U.S.A.   First Edition   10 9 8 7 6 5 4 3 2 1

With love to my daughter-in-law,
Ann Rendahl

CHAPTER 1

▼▼▼▼▼▼▼

"Your sister is coming," my mother cried, putting down the phone, "and there's nothing in the house to eat."

I stopped chewing my cheese-and-baloney sandwich. "Beth?" I said. "Beth is coming here?"

"And her mother, Mrs. Fancy Pants Lattimore," my mother cried. "Just like her—'Don't go to any trouble,' she says. 'We're at the airport, and we thought we'd just drop in for a little while. We're going to be staying at . . .' I forget—some fancy schmancy hotel in the city."

"But, Mom, how come they're not staying with us?"

My mother waved her hand impatiently. "Wait! Let me think for a minute. They're at the airport, so it should take them at least an hour before they get their stuff, rent a car. . . . You'd think she

1

could have let me know in advance, but that's the way she is . . . very mysterious . . . the great lady."

"Is Beth that way too?" I asked.

"Of course not," said my mother bitterly. "It's her mother. And you can be sure she'll expect lunch. You can be sure of that. What should I do? And the place is a mess. And your father's still sleeping?"

"I'll wake him up," I cried, "and he can go shopping. You'll tell him what to buy. Oh, it's so exciting." I knew my mother was upset. She was always upset when people dropped in without giving her notice. But I was thrilled. Beth, my sister, Beth, whom I hadn't seen for eight years, was coming to my house. Beth, my big sister, who was five years old the last time I'd seen her. Beth, whom I hardly remembered at all.

My mother was clutching her hands and moaning, "What should I give them for lunch? They're used to fancy cooking. What should I do?"

"I'll wake Daddy up. Maybe he'll have an idea."

"Oh him!" my mother cried, but I hurried off down the long, dark hall, shouting out the news before I reached my parents' bedroom.

"Beth's coming. Get up, Daddy. Hurry! Beth's coming with her mother. Hurry up! Get up!"

My father gulped down a cup of black coffee and tried to wake up. He drives a van for an airport shuttle company that services the downtown hotels, and he works the night shift. He doesn't get

2

home until six in the morning, and usually sleeps until two o'clock in the afternoon. Now it was only a little past noon, and he wasn't fully awake yet. But he was still trying to be helpful.

"You could make lasagna," he said sleepily. "You make the best lasagna."

"Are you crazy, Walter?" my mother snapped. "They'll be here in an hour. I don't have the time to make lasagna. It's got to be something quick but fancy."

"Oh!" My father took a few more gulps of his coffee. "Oh!"

"Pizza," I suggested. "We can get a few frozen pizzas at the market. I like the one with pepperoni. We could get one with pepperoni and one with sa-lami and . . . another one. I don't care as long as it doesn't have anchovies. Yuk! I hate anchovies."

"Don't be ridiculous," my mother cried. "We can't serve people like them frozen pizzas. They eat gourmet food—fancy things like artichokes and watercress."

"Chicken is always nice," my father suggested. "I can go to the deli and buy a barbecued chicken."

"And some macaroni salad," I suggested. "I love their macaroni salad."

"I don't know." My mother hesitated. "Do you think Mrs. Lattimore and Beth would eat macaroni salad?"

"I bet they'd like mushrooms," my dad said. "Don't rich people always like mushrooms?"

"That's right," my mother agreed. "Marinated

mushrooms, and maybe some of that smoked fish that costs twenty dollars a pound. I bet they'd like that."

"Let's just stick with the chicken," said my dad. "We don't have to turn the whole place upside down just because they're coming for lunch."

My father dressed quickly and hurried off with a long shopping list. While he was gone, my mother rushed through the apartment straightening up.

"Fresh flowers," my mother said. "I should have told him to buy some fresh flowers." She looked at the plants in front of the window in the living room and shook her head. "I don't know why we even bother with plants. There's just not enough light in this apartment."

"And you never remember to water them anyway."

"Well, I work a forty-hour week at Macy's, standing on my feet all day long, and come home and do all the cooking and cleaning . . ."

I made a face. I hated it when Mom started going on and on about how hard she worked as a saleswoman. It didn't happen too often, but it was boring whenever it did.

"Okay! Okay!" My mother stopped suddenly and turned to smile at me. One of her lower teeth had broken the day before yesterday while she was eating a piece of French bread, and she hadn't been able to get to the dentist. It gave her a funny smile. "Okay, Molly, don't mind me. I'm just a little flustered." She pulled me over, kissed my head, murmured that I was her pussycat girl, and I nuzzled her neck for a second before she started in again. "Okay, now I've got to get moving. I'll just get that plant out of the way." She pointed to a sick-looking rubber plant with a long skinny stem and a few yellowed speckled leaves on top.

"Where are you going to put it?"

"In my bedroom. They'll never go in there. I'll close the door."

It was a big, heavy plant, and she staggered as she carried it down the hall, shoved it into her bedroom, and slammed the door. When we came back into the living room, there was a big, ugly stain where the plant had stood, so then she had to move a bunch of other plants around before she was able to cover it.

"Beth's house has lots and lots of rooms," I told my mother.

She was busy pounding the cushions on the couch, trying to make them fluff up. They all had hollows in the center. "Next year," she muttered, "next year, we're going to get new furniture."

"They like old furniture, the Lattimores," I said. "Mrs. Lattimore wrote me at Christmas that they found some antiques for Beth's room. I think she said they were French or Italian. And they got an old marble washbasin for her bathroom. Beth has her own bathroom."

"Bathroom!" my mother yelled. "There's hair in the bathtub."

"There's always hair in the bathtub," I said, trailing after her. She began scrubbing out the tub, and I leaned against the door, watching her. After she finished with the tub, she began cleaning the sink and then the toilet. She changed the towels, the bathmat, and straightened up the toothbrushes.

"How come they're so rich?" I asked my mother. "Beth has her own bathroom, and her parents have their own bathroom, and I think Mrs. Lattimore said there are three more bathrooms in the house."

My mother was shaking her head up at the ceiling where some of the paint was cracking and curling. "We've got to get this place painted," she cried. "I just said to your father that as soon as I get a little money I'm going to get this place painted."

"But, Mom, how come they're so rich, and . . . and . . ." I didn't want to say *we're so poor* because I knew it would hurt my mother's feelings. But Beth and her parents lived in a house with five bathrooms and twelve other rooms while we lived in a house with five rooms and one bathroom. I was also pretty sure that Beth's family didn't have to wait until they had some extra money before they could paint their bathroom ceilings. I couldn't help feeling jealous of Beth.

"Lots of things aren't fair," my mother said. "Both of the Lattimores come from rich families. That's the way it is—some have it and some don't." Then she looked down at her watch and let out a yip. "We've got to get dressed. Hurry up!"

She followed me into my bedroom and stood with me in front of my closet.

"Should I wear a dress?" I asked. "Maybe the one I wore for Alex's wedding?"

"I don't know," my mother said doubtfully. "I think it's too hot today for that dress, and besides, I don't know if you should wear a dress. It's not like you're going to a party."

"Well, I haven't seen them for eight years."

"No!" My mother shut the closet door. "No dress! Casual. That's the best way. Just dress the way you always dress. People like them wouldn't be dressed up on an airplane anyway. I bet they're not worrying about what they're wearing."

"So what should I wear?"

"How about that cute little pair of red overalls you wear over your striped T-shirt?"

"No, it's too hot for that."

"Well, how about your white shorts and that little blue tank top I bought you last week?"

"The shorts are dirty."

It took a while, but finally, after trying on different combinations, I ended up wearing a pale pink tank top and a pair of lavender shorts.

"I don't know," I said, looking at myself in the mirror. "I don't know if the pink goes with the lavender."

My mother was smiling at me in the mirror. "Whatever you wear," she said in her mother voice, "you look cute."

"You always say that." I leaned back against her.

"But it's true," my mother said, smoothing my hair. "I'm not saying anything that's not so."

"I bet everybody's mother says the same thing about her own kid," I said. "Don't you think Mrs. Lattimore says the same thing about Beth?"

"Oh her!" my mother said scornfully.

My mother is always saying nasty things about Beth's mother. I don't know why because Mrs. Lattimore always writes nice letters to me and sends me great presents for Christmas and on my birthday. My father never says anything bad about her—only my mother does. I don't understand why.

For a long time, I couldn't understand why my sister Beth had one set of parents and I had another. It took me years to figure it out, but now that I'm eleven, I understand. It's not really complicated if you start at the beginning. Which is that Beth and I are sisters, and we had a different set of parents to begin with. I don't remember them at all. Beth told me in one of her letters that she does remember them, and that they were ugly. My mother says they weren't ugly. Sometimes she cries when she talks about them. She says Beth and I both look like our real mother, who was her younger sister, but I look especially like her.

I'd better start over again. Beth and I had the same parents, but one day when I was nearly three and Beth was five, we were all driving somewhere in our car, and a truck hit us. My mother and father were killed, Beth was hurt very badly, and I was crying when they got me out of the car, but I wasn't hurt. Sometimes I think I remember a loud, terrible crash, and somebody screaming and screaming and screaming, but usually it's just me screaming in the middle of the night. And then my mother rushes in and grabs me and rocks me and tells me it's all right and I'm her pussycat girl . . . and I go back to sleep.

So my mother, my present mother, isn't my real mother. She really is my aunt, my mother's older sister, my Aunt Karen and Beth's Aunt Karen. But she adopted me after the accident, and she says I began to call her Mommy and Uncle Walter Daddy, and she figured it would all work out for the best if I just went on calling them that.

My mother always talks about things working out for the best. She says that because Beth was hurt so badly, she had to spend a long time in the hospital, and needed a lot of special care. Mrs. Lattimore was a nurse in that hospital, and, according to my mother, she just went crazy over Beth because she had to spend so much time taking care of her, and, naturally, says my mother, Beth grew very attached to her. I know my mother must have been heartbroken over what finally happened, but she doesn't let on, and she just keeps saying that she guesses it all worked out for the best. She and my dad adopted me, and the Lattimores adopted Beth. Whatever she says, I'm pretty sure that she's never forgiven Mrs. Lattimore for taking Beth away. That's why she keeps saying nasty things about her.

I like to daydream sometimes about what would have happened if I had also been hurt in the accident and had to spend time in the hospital too. Would Mrs. Lattimore have wanted to adopt both of us? And what would it feel like to live in a house with twelve rooms and five bathrooms and be rich?

But for a long time I couldn't get it all straight. My father and mother tried, and my two brothers,

Jeff and Alex (who are also my cousins and Beth's cousins), tried, and finally, one day, Alex said he had a riddle for me. If I could figure out the riddle, he said, then I could figure out anything. This is the riddle:

> *Brothers and sisters I have none,*
> *but that man's father is my father's son.*

At first he wouldn't tell me the answer even though I cried, and Mom yelled at him, and Dad told him to shape up. He just laughed and said they should stop spoiling me and let me stand on my own two feet for a change.

My mom and dad would have told me the answer if they could have figured it out, but they couldn't either. Finally Alex did tell me, and I told my parents. Only it still took me a while to work out my own riddle. Most of my friends can't figure out Alex's riddle. Maybe I'll try it out on Beth. I bet she won't know the answer either.

CHAPTER 2

▼▼▼▼▼▼▼

By the time my father returned, Mom had the house pretty much straightened out. She and Dad laid the food out carefully on the good dishes. Mom even sprinkled parsley over the tops of the salads and added some stuffed olives for garnish.

"I wonder if we should eat in the dining room," Mom said.

"What's wrong with the kitchen?" my father demanded. "We always eat in the kitchen except when we have a big mob over."

"Well, Walter," my mother said, "people like the Lattimores probably eat all of their meals in the dining room."

"There's nothing wrong with eating in the kitchen," my father insisted. "When I was growing up, my family didn't even have a dining room."

"I don't have to use the fancy white tablecloth,"

11

Mom said. "I can use straw mats and—well—I guess we should use cloth napkins. They probably would never use paper napkins for company."

My father stood up and said in a cranky voice, "I'm going to go take a shower now—it's broiling outside, and I'm soaked."

"No!" my mother yelled. "Don't take a shower now. Wait until after they leave. I just cleaned the bathroom and put up fresh towels."

"I am going to take a shower now," my father said very slowly, his teeth clenched, "and then I am going to sit down in front of the fan in the living room and smoke a cigarette and read my paper until they come. And then I am going to eat my lunch in the kitchen. Is that clear?"

"Yes, Walter," my mother said, and we both watched his back as he stalked off to the bathroom.

"He hardly ever gets that way," my mother said in a low voice, "but maybe he's right. Maybe it would all work out for the best if we ate in the kitchen. I do have that cute little tablecloth Lisa gave me for Mother's Day. Remember? I know she got two of the same tablecloths as gifts when she and Alex got married, but it's all right. I don't mind. Remember, Molly? It's got six matching red napkins. We'll set out the food and the good dishes. It'll look nice. Daddy won't get upset if we use a tablecloth in the kitchen."

My mother set the table, and then I changed my outfit a couple more times. By the time Beth and her mother arrived, I was wearing a white-and-red shirt and a pair of red shorts. I was also wearing the little pearl earrings that my parents gave me for a birthday present when I turned eleven. That was back in February when they also let me get my ears pierced.

"I don't know if those earrings go with that outfit," my mother said.

"Well, I like them," I insisted, "and I want to wear them."

"Okay." My mother smiled. "If you want to wear the earrings, go ahead and wear them. On you, everything looks good." She patted her hair and inspected herself in the mirror. "How do you think I look?"

I came and stood next to her. We smiled at each other in the mirror, and my mom butted my head with her own. "We certainly do look alike," she said, "but you're really the image of . . . of . . ."

"Of Kathy?" I said, finishing the sentence. Kathy was her sister, my first mother. I never thought of her as Mom or Mother. I thought of her the way my mom thought of her—as Kathy, as Mom's younger sister.

"Well, of course, Kathy and I looked a whole lot alike, except she was smaller and prettier, the way you are."

I looked at our faces in the mirror. I guessed I was prettier than Mom, but she was old, nearly fifty, and her hair was gray, and she had wrinkles on her face and neck. But we both had the same dark eyes, the same kind of long nose and dark complexion. My hair was long and tied back in a ponytail.

"I used to have long hair too," said my mother, reaching over to pat my ponytail. "Only I wore it in braids, and so did Kathy." My mother started to laugh, and I did too. I knew what was coming. "She was such a brat. She hated to have her hair braided, and she used to scream bloody murder. All the neighbors could hear her." My mother shook her head, and I did too, remembering through her memories what a brat Kathy used to be.

"Of course, my mother didn't put up with any nonsense, and she'd just give her a good whack. So then Kathy would come crying to me, and I'd end up doing her hair. She said I didn't pull so hard, and I had those little pink ribbons I used to braid into her hair. Oh, she looked so cute with those pink ribbons in her hair . . ." Now my mother had tears starting up in her eyes, and I stopped looking into the mirror. I just put my arms around her waist and laid my head on her chest, and we stood there a couple of seconds. She tightened her arms around me. "You're so much like her," she murmured. And I didn't mind at all being compared to a dead, bratty girl.

"Okay, okay!" My mother pulled herself away. "Now tell me how I look."

She straightened herself up and made a half smile while she waited for me to say something.

"You look . . . you look . . ." What could I say? She was nearly fifty years old, she had wrinkles on her face and neck, a skinny body, and her clothes—a pink shirt and matching pants—hung on her like the skin on an unstuffed turkey. I thought of the last photo I'd received of Mrs. Lattimore—trim, smiling, and fashionable in her white tennis outfit with a white cardigan carelessly draped over her shoulders. My mother didn't play tennis, and her clothes didn't fit her the way Mrs. Lattimore's clothes fit her. What would it feel like to have a fashionable mother who played tennis and had a white cardigan draped carelessly over her shoulders? I knew it would feel wonderful. Guiltily, I looked at my own mother standing there, waiting for me to say something, a half smile on her face.

"You look fine," I told her.

"Well!" My mother turned to look at herself again in the mirror." I could wear a couple of gold chains around my neck. What do you think, Molly? Would they go?"

They didn't show up until nearly three. Mom had put the food in the refrigerator because she said it would spoil in all this heat. We took turns jumping up and going to the bathroom—Mom and I did. Dad just kept on smoking and reading his paper the way he said he would, and when he finished that, he leaned back in his chair and took a nap.

When the bell rang, he jumped up in his chair and said, "What? What?" the way he always did when he woke up suddenly from a nap.

"You go, Mom," I said. I felt shy suddenly.

"No, you go," she told me, turning toward the kitchen. "I'm going to take the food out of the refrigerator."

15

"Please, Mom," I whispered, "please. Let's go together."

"All right," she whispered back. "We'll go together."

They were standing there, outside the door, smiling at us and holding a bunch of flowers. That is, Mrs. Lattimore was smiling and holding a bunch of flowers. Beth wasn't smiling. Not doing anything. Just standing there and not looking at us.

"Well, hello," said Mrs. Lattimore. "It's so wonderful to see you again."

"Come in, come in," said my mother, and the two grown-ups began talking at the same time. ". . . So lucky you were home . . . wonderful that you had the time . . . exhausting trip . . . lunch . . . no trouble . . . terrible heat wave . . ."

Beth raised her eyes and looked at me. I looked back at her. Neither of us said anything. She was thirteen and at least half a head taller than me. She was also thin, with dark eyes, dark skin, and a long nose. Her hair, like mine, was dark but, unlike mine, it was cut short. She tossed it, and it made a wonderful wavy curve against her cheek. I broke down first and said, "Hi, Beth."

"Hi," she answered. I moved forward to kiss her cheek. She let me but stood still while I was doing it.

"Beth and I just couldn't wait to see you all," Mrs. Lattimore gushed, handing the flowers to Mom, "and just look at Molly. She's so . . . so . . . why, she and Beth look so much alike, don't they?"

16

"I need to go to the bathroom," Beth said.

"Oh, sure, honey," said my mother. "It's just down the hall and . . ."

"I know where it is," Beth said, moving quickly past my mother.

My mother looked after her, surprised, and Mrs. Lattimore said, "She really does have an amazing memory. I'm always astonished at the things she remembers."

"But she hasn't been here for . . . for . . ."

"It must be well over eight years," Mrs. Lattimore said, "but she can remember things that happened to her way before that."

My mother continued standing there looking after Beth. I said, "Hi, Mrs. Lattimore. Did you have a good trip?"

"Call me Aunt Helene," she said, bending down to give me a hug and kiss. "It was a lovely trip, and we brought you some surprises from Paris and London. Beth picked them out, but they're still in our suitcases. We'll get everything unpacked in our hotel later, and maybe one day . . ."

"Come in, come in." My mother had come to life again. "Come in. Walter's in the living room."

"Oh, how is he?" Aunt Helene moved down the hall, an arm around my shoulder. "And the boys? Just think—Alex is married. What's his wife like?"

"She's pregnant," I said, and Mom quickly added, "It was a very small wedding—just the immediate family—otherwise we would have . . ."

Dad was standing up when we walked into the living room, holding the paper.

"Well, Walter, how are you?" Aunt Helene

asked, dropping her arm from my shoulder and moving toward him. They shook hands, and both of them began talking at the same time. ". . . Fine . . . how's your husband? . . . sends regards . . . staying a few more weeks in London . . . broiling hot summer . . . several lectures . . . sit down, sit down . . . lunch in just a few minutes . . ."

"We've already eaten lunch." Beth stood at the door.

"Well, we just had a bite." Aunt Helene laughed. "I could certainly eat something else, but you shouldn't have gone to any trouble. Beth, come and say hello to your uncle."

"Hello." Beth remained standing at the door.

"Hello there, Beth," my father said. He hesitated for one moment and then walked over to her, bent down, and kissed her on the cheek. Beth stood still. Then my dad looked down at her and said, "Well, you certainly have grown into a young lady since the last time I saw you."

"Thank you," Beth said, not moving.

My father smiled, patted her shoulder, and continued. "You've changed a lot. You and Molly used to look a lot alike, but now I don't think you resemble each other at all."

"Thank you," Beth said, looking up at him and smiling for the first time.

"Oh, I think she looks a lot like Molly," said Aunt Helene.

My mother moved in slow motion over to Beth. Before, at the door, Beth had gone off to the bathroom so quickly, they hadn't really had a chance to kiss.

"Beth," my mother said, very softly, "I'm glad to see you, Beth." She bent over and tried to kiss her right cheek, but Beth turned her head away so quickly that the kiss landed on her left cheek.

It made me angry to see how rude Beth was to my mom. I knew how much my mother suffered because Beth had chosen to be adopted by the Lattimores rather than by her own family. I knew, even though my mother never blamed Beth, how all these years she must have felt rejected and hurt. She should have been the one who turned away from Beth's kiss instead of the other way around. It made me angry, and it made me feel guilty, too, for some of my own daydreams about living with the Lattimores. And as the grown-ups, for the first time, stood around silently, I shouted out at Beth, "I know a riddle I bet you don't know."

"What is it?"

I told her. "Brothers and sisters I have none, but that man's father is my father's son."

"Oh," she said, "everybody knows that one. *That man* is the son of the person who's speaking."

CHAPTER 3

▼▼▼▼▼▼

As soon as we sat down around the kitchen table, Beth pointed up at the window and asked, "What happened to the curtains?"

All of us looked at the window, which was covered by a white blind. Right now the blind was raised to let in the air because it was such a hot day. Usually, we pull it down because all you can see from that window is the kitchen window in the house next door.

"Curtains?" my mother repeated. "What curtains?"

"You had curtains with vegetables on them," Beth said. "There were carrots and green peppers and tomatoes."

"Oh?" My mother's face drew in as she thought. "Oh . . . yes . . . but that must have been ten years ago at least."

"They were here eight years ago," Beth corrected, picking up her plate. "I remember them when I came back from the hospital after the accident."

"I don't remember them," I said.

Beth turned the dish in her hand. "And you had different dishes. They had green flowers on them, big green flowers with red leaves."

My mother didn't say anything, but my father laughed. "What a memory you have, Beth. You're right about those dishes. I think I liked them better than the ones we have now."

"I like these better," I said, looking at my mother's face.

"This is just delicious." Aunt Helene picked up a small piece of bread. "That's one thing about New York. The bread is really wonderful here. Beth, try a piece."

"I'm not hungry," Beth said, "but I am thirsty."

My mom leaped up. "What would you like? I have Coke, 7-up, milk . . ."

"Do you have lemonade?"

"No, but . . ."

Beth shrugged. "I'll just have water then."

"I can make you some lemonade," my mother said. "I mean, if there are lemons . . . I can't remember if I have any lemons." She opened the refrigerator door and began rummaging around inside.

"Oh please, Karen," Aunt Helene said, "don't bother. Beth is kind of a fussy eater."

"I am not a fussy eater," Beth said. "I just like

lemonade, but I'm perfectly willing to drink water."

My mother held up a lemon and a half. "Here," she said breathlessly, "I can make you some."

"Please don't bother, Karen," Aunt Helene said.

"It's no bother at all." My mother began frantically opening and closing the drawers of the cupboard as she searched for the juicer. We hardly ever squeeze lemons in my family.

"So—how was Europe?" my dad asked as my mother noisily moved things around.

"The weather was terrible," Aunt Helene said, "especially in Paris. If you think it's hot here—it was just broiling there, and London—I think it rained almost every day. It's good to be back. Poor John is still in England. He has to give a few more lectures. Suddenly the whole world is interested in eighteenth- and nineteenth-century American painters."

"Is that so?" inquired my father, trying to look interested.

"Oh, yes!" Aunt Helene nodded her head up and down. "When he went into the field, there was absolutely no interest at all, and nobody wanted to publish his first book. Now"—she took a tiny bite of the piece of bread in her hand—"now he has three major publishers trying to outbid each other for his next book."

My mother found the juicer and began squeezing the lemon and a half.

"I don't like any of the lemon pieces," Beth said. "I like to have my lemonade strained."

My mother stopped squeezing the lemons and began opening and closing the drawers of the cupboard again as she looked for the strainer. We eat the kind of meals in my house that don't require juicers or strainers.

"Are you going right back to California?" my father asked.

"No. I thought we'd run up to Maine for a week or so. You know my sister and her family live there. We haven't seen her since Christmas—she and the kids were out to see us then. We usually visit back and forth a couple of times a year. We're very close."

Beth and I looked at each other. I wondered if she was thinking the same thing I was thinking. In the eight years since we were separated, we hadn't seen each other—not even once. Not that I had missed her, the way I sometimes do miss my brothers. But I'd always wanted to go to California and stay in Beth's big, rich house and play with all her toys and see for myself if they really had five bathrooms.

"I don't want to go to Maine," Beth said.

My mother brought Beth her lemonade and placed it in front of her. She had filled one of the tall, fancy, pink glasses and set it down on a saucer. It looked delicious with the ice glistening inside it. My mother's face was red and wet with perspiration. She stood there waiting as Beth picked up the glass, sipped it, made a face, and said, "It's not sweet enough." I noticed that Beth had a gold charm bracelet on her wrist with tiny little charms that quivered as she moved her arm.

"Well . . ." My mother hurried off to find the sugar bowl and set it down before Beth. "Here, Beth, just add some more sugar—as much as you like."

"Sit down, Karen," Aunt Helene urged. "Beth is fine. It was very sweet of you to go to all that trouble for her. At home she usually makes her own lemonade."

I watched Beth add one . . . two . . . three teaspoons of sugar. She tasted her lemonade after each addition while my mother stood there, waiting. Finally, after the third teaspoon, Beth set down her spoon and began sipping. Then my mother sat down. Beth didn't say thank you to my mother or smile at her. She just drank her lemonade with a sour face, and I decided that I didn't like Beth.

"So—Karen, tell us about Alex's wife. Her name's Lisa, isn't it?"

"She's pregnant," I said again.

"Will you stop that!" my mother snapped. She turned to Aunt Helene. "She's . . . well . . . she's very nice, I guess. Very intelligent." My mother said the word *intelligent* in a way that meant she really didn't think Lisa was intelligent. "They both met at college only . . . only now Alex had to stop and find a job. I mean since they got married."

I could hear the bitterness in my mother's voice. Alex is the smartest one of the three of us. A straight-A student all through school, and only a year to go before he would have finished college and gotten his degree in mathematics. We all expected him to go on to graduate school, but all of a sudden, he and Lisa decided to get married.

"He'll go back," my father said, trying to sound cheerful. "Maybe he can finish at night. It's all right."

"Alex also has a good singing voice, doesn't he?" Aunt Helene asked.

"No, Mom, I keep telling you." Beth put down her glass of lemonade. "Jeff is the one who sings. He's older. He's twenty-four, and Alex is twenty-one—only eight years older than I."

"Oh, that's right," Aunt Helene said. "Well, Karen and Walter, I wish them both lots of luck, but I do agree with Karen that it's better to finish your education before you marry. John and I waited until he finished his degree."

I wanted to repeat that Lisa was pregnant and that was why they had to get married because Aunt Helene didn't seem to understand. But my mother had a strained look on her face, so I kept quiet.

"Jeff had a beautiful voice," Beth said. "He always said he was going to be a singer."

"He still does," my mother said grimly.

"He always knew lots of songs." Beth turned to me for the first time. "Does he still know lots of songs?"

"Oh, sure," I told her. "He's always coming up with new songs. He's the only one in the family who sings. Nobody else can carry a tune."

"I can carry a tune," Beth said.

"Actually, Beth has a lovely voice," her mother

said. "She's quite a musician. You should hear her on the piano. Her teacher thinks she could be a professional if she wanted." Aunt Helene laughed. "John and I love music, but neither of us has much talent. I studied piano for years, but I never could play as well as Beth."

My mother cleared her throat. "Molly could have played too," she began, but my father interrupted, shaking his head.

"She didn't want to practice," he said.

"Now, Walter," my mother protested, "that's not exactly true. You remember that was the year she had all those colds, and she just didn't have the energy."

"Nothing can stop Beth from practicing," her mother said. "Even when she's sick, she'll get up and practice. I remember once when she had chicken pox . . ."

Aunt Helene went on and on, bragging about what a prodigy Beth was. I felt like throwing up. Beth was pretending to examine the little charms on her bracelet, and she was smiling. My sister was turning out to be a real drag.

My sister? It was hard for me to think of Beth as part of my family. I watched her pick up her lemonade and begin sipping it again. Even though she had the same dark eyes and the same dark skin and the same long nose—even though she looked kind of like me and my mom, and even though my mom was her aunt and my aunt too, and my brothers were her cousins and my cousins too—she didn't feel like a part of my family.

Her mother stopped talking.

Beth looked at me suddenly and asked, "Are there still two beds in your room?"

"Two beds?"

"Well, you're sleeping in Jeff and Alex's old room, aren't you?"

"Yes, now I am."

"They used to have a trundle bed in their room, and sometimes when we slept over, we slept there, and the boys slept on the pullout couch in the living room. Do you still have that trundle bed?"

I looked over at my mom. Her face was pale and unhappy. I knew she must be thinking of how Beth chose to go with the Lattimores instead of staying with us. How she had her own big room in San Francisco instead of sharing my small bedroom and the trundle bed.

"Yes," I said to her coldly, "I still have that trundle bed."

Beth finished her glass of lemonade and stood up. "Let's go see your room," she said.

Her mother looked down at her watch and said, "Beth, we should be going soon."

"Why?" Beth asked over her shoulder as she headed toward the door.

"We need to check in at the hotel. I said we'd be there before six."

Beth turned. "Can't you call from here and tell them we'll be coming later?"

My mother cleared her throat. "Are you staying in the city tonight?" She had that nervous look, which meant she would have liked to invite them to stay over but was worried about where to put them.

"Actually," said Aunt Helene, "we'll be staying three or four nights. John wants me to meet with some of the publishers and also to check out a few museums . . ." Her voice drifted off. "We'll probably take off for Maine next Tuesday or Wednesday."

"Boring!" Beth said, standing in the doorway. "I hate museums, and I hate Maine."

"Now, darling," her mother said, "maybe we can manage to go to a few concerts. It's hard for Beth to be away from the piano for so long," she said, turning to my parents.

"They don't have a piano in Maine," Beth said. "And the kids are a bunch of jocks. There's nothing to do in Maine."

"We'll go swimming," her mother said.

"The water's too cold."

"You're just tired, darling, after the trip. Why don't we go on to the hotel right now, and maybe you can take a nap."

"I'm not tired," Beth said, sounding very cranky, "and I don't want to go to the hotel yet. I want to see Molly's room. You dragged me here. I didn't want to come, but now that I'm here, you're not letting me have any fun."

Nobody else was having any fun either. It was embarrassing, the mean way Beth was talking to her mother. My mother got up and began shuffling the plates around, my Dad lit a cigarette, and I looked over at the window and tried to remember those curtains with the vegetables on them.

"Well, all right, Beth," said Aunt Helene. "You go off with Molly for a little while. As long as it's okay with your Aunt Karen and Uncle Walter, that is."

"Absolutely," my dad said.

"You're sure we're not taking up your time?"

"No, no, no!" my mother insisted. "We can just have something cool to drink while the girls play. Would you like some Coke or 7-up or . . ."

"Anything," we heard Aunt Helene say as Beth and I moved out of the kitchen.

"Play!" Beth muttered. "She must think we're two-year-olds."

You're acting like a two-year-old, I wanted to say, but I didn't. She made me uncomfortable, and I couldn't figure her out. Why was she so mean and nasty when she had so many things other people didn't? I couldn't understand her at all, but I did understand that her family was a lot richer than mine, that she got to go to places like France and England and Maine, that she lived in a big, wonderful house in San Francisco, and that her hair was short and moved in a beautiful curve whenever she shook her head. And her clothes—both her clothes and her mother's clothes—were expensive, designer clothes that made me feel my mother and I were wearing rags. I felt angry and jealous and I wanted her to go away. She and her fashionable mother.

She moved quickly ahead of me down the hall to my room as if she knew exactly where it was. At the door she paused for a moment, looking around.

"It's such a little room," she said. "I forgot that it was so little."

"It's not so little," I said.

"And you have a different spread on the bed. The boys had a dark blue one with a spot in the middle."

"I picked out the spread," I said proudly. "Mom . . . my mom . . . let me pick it out last Christmas. It matches the curtains, and just a couple of months ago, my dad and I painted the room and put up the wallpaper."

"Pink!" Beth wrinkled up her face. "All that pink! I hate pink."

"Well, I like it," I told her, but she was not listening.

She moved over to the bed and stood there, looking down at it. "Pull it out," she ordered.

"Why should I?"

She didn't answer. She just bent over, reached underneath, and pulled out the trundle bed. Then she looked around the room again. "It is a very small room," she said.

"I don't think it's small," I said angrily. "Maybe it's not as big as your room, but it was plenty big enough for both of the boys, and it would have been big enough for . . . for . . ."

Beth suddenly dropped down on my bed. Not the trundle bed but my bed, right on top of my beautiful, frilly, pink spread.

"You've got your shoes on my spread," I yelled.

She kicked them off and stretched herself. "I used to sleep here," she said, "on this bed. I used to sleep here."

"When did you ever sleep here?" I demanded.

"Then," she said. "Before the accident. I slept on this bed, and you slept on the trundle bed."

"I don't remember."

"Lie down," she ordered. "Go ahead. Lie down."

"No."

She sat up and looked at me with a different kind of look. "Please, Molly, lie down. Please."

"Okay, okay," I grumbled. I lay down on the trundle bed. It was narrower than my bed but it was okay. "There's nothing wrong with the trundle bed," I said. "My friends sleep over all the time."

"Good for them."

I looked over at my pretty pink curtains. "I love pink," I said.

"I hate it."

"You keep saying you hate everything," I told her angrily. "What do you like? Is there anything you like?"

"I like plenty of things," she said. "But you have to be stupid to like everything the way you do."

"I don't like everything."

"Okay—tell me what you don't like."

You, I wanted to say, you. But I held back, thinking, and while I did, Beth said, looking up at the ceiling, "There used to be another fixture on that light."

"Yes," I agreed, "a big, ugly one."

"It looked like a saucer. I was just a little kid then but I remember it looked like a saucer, and I used to wonder what was inside it."

"I picked this one out when we painted."

31

She wasn't listening. "I didn't want to come today," she said. "I never wanted to come back, even though my mom thought I should. But I can remember how we used to sleep over sometimes when our parents had a night out, and I used to love it then. The boys were so sweet—especially Jeff."

"They still are. Alex is sweet too, but Lisa is a real crab, and—"

"And Uncle Walter was nice even though he was so big and had such a deep voice, and even *she* . . . even *she* was okay. I remember *she* bought me a doll once . . . I liked her a lot then."

"So why aren't you nicer to her now?" I demanded. "You were the one who made her feel bad when you went away with the Lattimores. Why are you so mean to her? Why are you so nasty? Don't you know you make her feel bad? Don't you know she loves you a lot, and if you had decided to stay, she would have done anything for you?"

Beth didn't answer. She was asleep.

CHAPTER 4

▼▼▼▼▼▼

"She's asleep," I told them. The grown-ups were still sitting around the table, my parents drinking Cokes and Aunt Helene sipping a glass of ice water.

"Sleeping!" Aunt Helene stood up. "She's really exhausted. We probably should have come another day, but you're so close to the airport, and we . . . we were looking forward to seeing you."

"Why don't you let her nap for a while?" my father suggested.

"No, I'd better wake her. Once she falls asleep, she'll sleep through the whole night. Where's the bedroom?"

My mother led her down the hall, and I followed along behind them.

"Well, isn't this a pretty room." Aunt Helene stood in the doorway, looking in.

"I picked out the spread and the curtains and the wallpaper."

"A real girl's room." Aunt Helene smiled at me. "Such pretty shades of pink!" She moved over to the bed. Beth was lying on her side, facing the wall, the way I slept. It felt funny seeing her on my bed, sleeping the way I always slept. Aunt Helene put a hand on her hair and began smoothing it.

"Beth dear, Bethy . . ." she murmured.

Beth didn't wake up.

"She's a very heavy sleeper," Aunt Helene said. "She could sleep through an earthquake."

"Molly's the same way," said my mom.

"Beth, dear . . . Beth . . ."

Beth curled herself up into a tight knot.

"Wake up, dear! We have to go now. Beth!"

Suddenly, Beth rolled over onto her back, opened her eyes, and blinked up at the ceiling.

"We have to go now, dear," her mother said softly. "You can take a little nap in the car if you're still tired."

"No!" Beth said.

"We'll get to the hotel as fast as we can, darling, and you can go right to bed if you like, or maybe we can order something up from room service."

Beth looked up at the three of us standing by the bed, and tears began rolling down her face.

"Beth!" Her mother sat down and tried to put her arms around her. "It's all right, darling, it's all right. You're just a little tired and . . ."

Beth shook her off. "I want to stay here," she

34

sobbed, the tears streaming down her face. "I don't want to go."

She sounded like a little girl. She didn't sound anything like Beth.

"But, darling, you know we have plans. If you don't like them, we can do other things."

"I want to stay here," Beth cried.

"Maybe," my mother said nervously, "you can both stay over. We do have a couch that opens up in the living room."

"That's very sweet of you," Aunt Helene said, "but I really need to get to the hotel. My husband will be calling us this evening, and I have some other arrangements I need to make. Please, Beth!"

"I want to stay here," Beth cried. "You go and let me stay."

"Well . . ." my mother said slowly, "well . . . of course . . ."

"Please, Mom!" Beth sat up and snuggled against her mother's shoulder. "Please! You always wanted me to come back."

"Dear, I just don't know if your aunt and uncle . . ."

"Oh, sure." My mother laughed in a strange, nervous way. "Beth is always welcome here. Of course, we'd love to have her, and maybe Walter can drop her off tomorrow."

"Can I see Jeff?" Beth turned toward my mother while her mother practically picked her up onto her lap and curled her arms around her.

"Well, I don't know," my mother said. "I can try to call him, but I don't know what he's doing today."

"And Alex too? Can I see him . . . and Lisa?" Beth sounded so eager and excited that my mother turned away, embarrassed. "I'll call them. I don't know . . ."

"Mom." Beth looked up into her mother's face. "Mom, I want to stay. Please!"

Her mother kissed her and murmured, "Of course, sweetheart. As long as it's all right with your aunt."

"Oh, sure," said my mother, straightening up some papers on my desk.

"But Beth . . ." Aunt Helene hesitated. "Are you sure? You know, we could come back another day, or maybe Molly could meet us in the city. Maybe she could even come back with us today, and tomorrow the three of us could have a day in town. We could have lunch at the Russian Tea Room, and—"

"I want to stay here, Mom. I really want to stay here."

"Well . . ." Aunt Helene looked over toward my mother's back as she continued straightening the papers on my desk. "I guess I could come back and get you tomorrow."

"That's right," Beth said. "Tomorrow! And maybe if Jeff—and Alex and Lisa too—if they can't come today, they can come tomorrow. You could see them. You'd meet Lisa—we'd both meet Lisa."

My mother turned, a look of disgust on her face. She didn't think meeting Lisa was such a big deal.

"Now, Karen, are you absolutely sure?"

"Of course," said my mother. I could see that she wasn't happy to have Beth stay overnight, and I knew why. It would bring back all those old sad memories of the accident, and how Beth had turned away from us all and chose to go and live with the Lattimores.

A year and a half ago, Aunt Helene had called before Christmas and invited me to spend the holidays with them out in California. Mom didn't want me to go. She put down the receiver in disgust and muttered something about fancy ladies making a nuisance of themselves. Alex was still home then, and all of us were eating dinner in the kitchen while Mom talked on the phone.

"What was that all about?" Alex asked.

"It's her, the great lady. She's on my neck again."

"What does she want?" My dad helped himself to another hamburger.

"She wants Molly to go out to California by herself and spend the holidays with them."

"I want to go," I yelled. "Lots of kids my age go on planes by themselves. And they have a big, beautiful house with lots of toys, and Mrs. Lattimore says Beth has her own bathroom, and she has a great big dollhouse."

"You have a dollhouse too," said my mother angrily.

"But Mrs. Lattimore says Beth's dollhouse has lights that go on and off, and a little refrigerator that gets cold, and you can actually keep food in it. Mrs. Lattimore says she has a dollhouse family made out of china, and there's a little Jacuzzi . . ."

They were all quiet, watching me. Finally, Alex asked, "Why do they want Molly now, after all these years?"

"Something about a therapist thinking it's a good idea," said my mom, still angry. "Naturally, she tried to act like they're dying to have Molly out, but they've never shown much interest before."

"Mrs. Lattimore calls me sometimes," I reminded her, "and she sends me birthday presents, and every Christmas they send all of us beautiful presents."

"We send them beautiful presents too," said my dad. "A lot more beautiful and expensive than we should, but your mother has a bee in her bonnet about keeping up with the Lattimores."

"For God's sake, Walter," my mother yelled, "they sent us all cashmere sweaters last year. What am I supposed to do? Send them a calendar?"

"Yes," my dad said. "They're in another league from us financially. You don't have to be ashamed of what you are."

"Can I go?" I asked. "I want to go."

"No," said my mother. "You're going to stay home. We'll have Christmas dinner here with the family."

"I want to go!" I yelled. "I want to go! I want to go!"

"I think she should go," Alex said. "It's not right to keep the girls apart. That's probably what the therapist said."

"I don't care what the therapist said," my

mother yelled. "Molly is too young to go by herself."

There was a lot of yelling, crying, and slamming of doors, as there often is whenever my family discusses something controversial. But I know how to handle my mother, and generally I get my way.

"Stop babying her," Alex always used to say to her. "She's a spoiled brat, and it's your fault. You never babied us the way you do her. We always had to pick up after ourselves, and we always had chores. She doesn't lift a finger around here, and she always gets anything she wants."

Jeff says that Alex was always a little jealous of me. He says Alex was the baby before I came to live with them. I can't remember because I was only three at the time, and my brothers always seemed like grown-ups to me.

Maybe Alex picks on me sometimes, but I can always handle my mom. I just stop talking to her. She can't ignore me for more than a day. Then she'll follow me around and try to reason with me. Maybe she'll try to bargain. But if I can keep up the silent treatment long enough, she'll give in.

Not that year. I cried and stopped talking to her for a week. She went through the first two stages—ignoring me and reasoning with me. But she didn't give in. I heard her crying one night in her bedroom, and my dad said, "Maybe you ought to let her go, Karen. Maybe it would be all for the best."

She just cried louder, but I didn't get to go.

We sent fancy presents, though—gold cuff links

for Mr. Lattimore, a big red silk scarf for Mrs. Lattimore, and a gold locket for Beth.

I didn't talk much to my mom for a while. I was polite but cold. Alex took me to see *The Nutcracker* ballet and treated me to lunch in the city. Even though he's the one in the family who picks on me the most, he's also the one who spends—well, before Lisa, he used to spend—the most time with me. While we were eating, he gave me one of his big-brother lectures. I didn't mind. I was used to them, and I was enjoying myself too much.

"You have to understand that Mom has had enough problems in her life."

"Umm," I said, and poured more ketchup over my French fries.

"You're not a baby anymore, even if she treats you like one, and you're old enough to stop making her feel bad."

I swallowed a couple of fries.

"I thought you should have gone out to San Francisco too," he said, "but Mom isn't ready for you to go. Just hang on another couple of years and try to understand."

I licked some ketchup off my mouth. At that moment, I didn't mind not going to San Francisco. I was having too good a time with my brother Alex. And I did understand. It was because of Beth. Because she had chosen to go off to live with the Lattimores, and my mother was afraid the same thing would happen to me. She was afraid I might decide to go stay with them too.

In my daydreams I used to wonder about that

myself. What would I do if they asked me? Maybe they'd say something like, "Molly, we'd really like you to come and live with us too. You could have your own big room with all the toys you'd like, and your own bathroom, and a dollhouse just like Beth's. And you could come with us to London and Paris and Maine." Well, of course, I'd thank them very much, but I'd say no. I think I'd say no.

So that night, I started talking to my mom again. I sat on her lap, and she laughed and said what would I like to do very, very special during the holidays.

"Have a slumber party," I told her.

She didn't put up any kind of fuss. Four of my friends stayed over. We all slept on the floor in the living room, and we made such a racket all night long that Mrs. Palagonia from upstairs banged on the ceiling. My mom didn't say a word. She made us frozen waffles and bacon for breakfast, and later that week, she let me buy a bunch of new outfits for my Barbie doll.

CHAPTER 5

▼▼▼▼▼▼

My mother was too busy complaining in a low voice about having to make dinner on Sunday to listen to me.

"I was looking forward to taking it easy this weekend, just doing nothing for a change, maybe even going to the beach, maybe sitting under a tree in the park, maybe just staying home and relaxing . . ."

"She's sleeping in my bed," I told them. My dad was sitting in front of the fan, smoking and listening to my mom.

"So now I have to make dinner for nine people. Of course, Jeff has to bring over a friend—some girl named Ginger—and it's going to be another blazing hot day . . . I need all this like a hole in the head."

"She won't move," I said. "She's sleeping in my bed, and she won't move."

My mother waved a hand at me to shut up, to stop interrupting her while she was in the midst of something important. "I'll have to go shopping tomorrow, and I'll have to spend the whole day cooking . . ."

"I'll help," my dad said sympathetically. "I'll go out shopping early in the morning, and—"

"I don't even know what to make," my mother cried, but in a low voice.

"Lasagna," both of us said together and smiled at each other. Lasagna was my mother's greatest triumph—she wasn't that good a cook otherwise, but nobody ever made lasagna the way she did. Nobody.

"It's too hot," my mother complained. "Who needs the oven on when the temperature is in the 90's? And who wants to eat lasagna on a miserably hot day?"

"I could eat your lasagna on any kind of day," my father said. "I could eat your lasagna on a hot day or on a cold day." He paused, shook his head up and down, and added, "And I could eat your lasagna hot or cold or . . ." Another pause. "Or room temperature. Nobody makes lasagna like you."

My mother lifted her chin, but she still pretended to be undecided. "And what about dessert?"

"Can we have a German chocolate cake from Kings?" I said.

"Well—I don't know if Beth likes chocolate cake. And Mrs. Lattimore—she's probably one of those people who doesn't eat sweets at all."

"Who cares?" said my dad. "We like chocolate cake—right, Molly? So that's what we'll have."

"I suppose we could always pick up some straw-berries too," my mother said. "People like Mrs. Lattimore always seem to like strawberries. And I'll make lemonade." My mother nodded and began to look comfortable. "We'll get up early and do the shopping, and I'll start the sauce and then assemble the lasagna. I'll just have to pop it in the oven for forty minutes, and maybe we can ask Alex to bring over his fan. Okay, if you really want me to, I'll make lasagna."

That settled, I could get back to my problem. "She's sleeping on my bed," I said. "She took a shower, and then I guess I was on the phone to Cindy, and when I got back to my room, she was asleep on my bed. And she won't wake up."

"I made up the trundle bed for her," Mom said.

"I know you did. I even showed her that you put on a brand-new sheet and a new pillowcase—in blue and white since she kept saying how much she hated pink. She knew you were making up the trundle bed for her."

"Don't make a big deal of it," my dad advised. "It's only for one night."

"She did it on purpose," I said, "just to be mean. She's the meanest kid I ever met."

"No, no," said my mother. "It's not her. It's her mother. She's the one who . . . who . . ."

The three of us drew together and spoke in whispers.

"She seems nice to me," said my dad. "A little wishy-washy but I think she really cares for Beth. And I think Beth is happy although she is kind of crabby . . ."

"I guess it all worked out for the best," said my mother, looking very, very tired.

"Did you see the bracelet Beth was wearing?" I asked them. "It's a charm bracelet, and every charm is different and—"

"Now you stop that!" said my mother. "You just stop it!"

"Stop what?"

"Just stop it! I think it's crazy to let a kid wear an expensive piece of jewelry anyway. She could lose it or somebody might steal it."

"I bet she never takes it off," I told them. "I wouldn't if I had a bracelet like that."

"I'm warning you," my mother snapped. "You just cut it out!"

"Karen! Karen!" my father murmured. "Molly didn't mean anything. You can't blame her for admiring something beautiful."

"It has a gold heart with a tiny diamond. When she moves her arm, it flashes, and then there's a little . . ."

"All right now—that's enough!" Now it was my father snapping at me.

"It's her mother's fault," said my mom. "She probably gives her anything she wants."

I thought about Beth as I lay on the trundle bed later that night. My window was wide open, and the curtains were tied back, but there was no breeze stirring. My pillow heated up, and I kept turning it over and over to find a cool spot.

Beth slept. Even though I thumped my pillow around and muttered out loud on purpose about how hot it was, she went right on sleeping, curled up and facing the wall, the way I did.

Why was she here in the first place? And why was she so mean in the second place? I turned my pillow over and found one small, coolish spot over near the bottom which quickly warmed up after I lay my hot face on it. And why was she especially mean to my mom in the third place?

I determined that I wouldn't let her get away with making my mother feel bad anymore. If she said one more mean thing, I would . . . I would . . . my pillow grew so warm that I just tossed it on the floor and fell asleep finally without it.

"Molly! Molly! Are you awake, Molly?"

"No," I said.

"Molly, listen, Molly. I want to tell you something."

I opened my eyes. It was dark, and the clock on my bureau said 3:32.

"Are you crazy?" I asked her. "It's the middle of the night. I want to sleep."

"I guess I'm still on English time," she said, sounding a little bit sorry. "But I have to tell you something."

"I don't want to hear it," I said, feeling my hot, heavy eyelids shutting. "Tell me in the morning. I can't listen now. I can't . . ."

As soon as I woke up the next morning, I turned toward my bed. Beth wasn't in it. The clock said 9:07. I jumped up and hurried down the hall to the bathroom. I could hear voices from the kitchen, so I washed up, combed my hair, and went back up the hall.

Beth was sitting in the kitchen, talking to my father. Both of them were smiling. My mother was nowhere in sight.

"Good morning, Merry Sunshine," said my father cheerfully. "Beth and I are arguing about politics."

"Where's Mom?"

"Oh, she insisted on going out to pick up some muffins for breakfast and some lemons. She'll be back soon."

"The U.N. has to play a bigger role in world politics," Beth announced.

"The U.N.?" My father laughed. "The U.N. is just a big debating society."

"It's much better to debate," Beth leaned forward, "than to wage war. People get killed in a war—children too."

"Well," said my father, nodding, "you're right, of course, but I'm afraid until human beings change we'll always have war. Anyway, I'm really impressed, Beth. You certainly take an interest in things, and you seem to know what's happening out in the world. I wish . . ." My father left the sentence unfinished, but glanced quickly at me and then away. I knew what he was thinking. He was thinking that he was the only one who read the newspaper and that neither my mom nor I showed any interest at all in what was happening to the rest of the world. It made me feel angry and jealous.

"Then human beings will just have to change," Beth said.

"It's hot," I complained. "I'm going to take a shower."

"Good idea," my father agreed as he leaned forward and continued talking to Beth.

By the time I had taken my shower and dressed myself in a pink shirt, pink shorts, and pink socks, my mother had returned and was bustling around the kitchen. I could hear her chattering away even before I entered the room.

". . . Whatever you like, Beth. I bought a bunch of lemons, and I can make you some lemonade."

"I don't drink lemonade in the morning," Beth said. She wasn't smiling anymore. She was looking over at the kitchen window, and her face had its usual mean look on it. My father was no longer in the room.

"Oh!" My mother said nervously. "Then what? . . ."

"Oh, I just like milk with a touch of nutmeg in it." Beth continued looking at the window.

"Nutmeg?" My mother took a breath. "I'm not sure I have any nutmeg."

"Water then," Beth said as if she were talking to a waitress. "I'll just have some water."

My mother hesitated and then said softly to Beth, "Your mother was a fussy eater too when she was a child."

"No, she was not," Beth said firmly, her eyes still on the window. "She wasn't a fussy eater when she was a child, and she isn't one now either."

"I meant . . . I meant your real mother."

"Well, so did I," Beth said fiercely, turning and glaring now at my mother.

"What is the matter with you?" I yelled at Beth. "She meant Kathy. You know very well she meant Kathy. You just stop picking on her."

Beth turned to look at me. "What do you know?" she asked. "You don't know anything."

"I know plenty," I said. "I know you're mean and selfish, and you're making my mother feel bad."

"She's not your mother," Beth cried in a shrill voice. "She's your aunt."

"Well, if she's not my mother," I yelled, "Aunt Helene isn't your mother either."

Beth stood up, and the two of us moved toward each other. Oh, I thought, if I could just land one punch on her mean face, and get one grab at her shiny, short hair . . .

But my mom got between us and put a hand on each of our shoulders.

"No!" she said. "No!"

The three of us stood there straining against one another, and then my father came into the room.

"What's going on here?" he asked. "What's all the yelling about?"

"She picked on Mom," I yelled.

"She insulted me," Beth cried.

"Girls! Girls! Girls!" said my mother.

"You know what?" said my dad, laughing. "I think we need to call in the U.N. Right, Beth?"

And then Beth began laughing too. My father put his arm around her shoulder, and she leaned against him. "I'm sorry, Uncle Walter," she said.

"You should apologize to my mother," I told

her, "not to my dad. She's the one you should apologize to."

"Let's just start all over again," my father said. "Let's have breakfast, and then the two of you can come shopping with me. We're going to have the whole gang over later, and Beth, you haven't tasted anything until you've tasted your Aunt Karen's lasagna."

Beth made a face. "I don't like lasagna," she said.

"Oh, you'll like *this* lasagna," said my dad.

My mother was rummaging around in the cupboard and held up a small box. "Here, Beth. See? I do have nutmeg."

"Maybe I'll get dressed first," Beth said to my dad. "The three of you are already dressed."

"Good idea!" My dad patted her shoulder, smiled, and watched her as she walked off down the hall. Then he turned to me. He wasn't smiling. "Molly," he said, "I don't like the way you're acting."

"Me?" I protested. "She started it. Didn't she, Mom?"

But my mother only shook her head and began putting the muffins into a basket. My mother hardly ever remains silent during an argument, and I watched her in surprise.

"I don't care who started it." My father took me by the arm and spoke in a very low voice.

"She insulted Mom. She—"

"Beth is your sister," my father interrupted, "and she's also your guest."

"She's not my guest. I didn't invite her."

My father shook my arm and said angrily but

still in a very low voice, "Now, I want you to cut it out. Do you hear me? I want you to cut it out and behave yourself. If you talk nicely to her, she'll talk nicely to you. I really enjoyed my conversation with her this morning. She's a very intelligent, interesting girl—and she knows what's happening in the world."

"She's a stinker, and she's mean to Mom."

Suddenly, my mother broke in. "Listen to your father, Molly," she said. "You just do what he tells you."

"Mom," I cried. "She was rude to you, she—"

"All right now, Molly." My father tightened his grip on my arm. "I want you to go and apologize to Beth."

"No," I said, "I won't."

"Oh, yes, you will." My father began moving me toward the door. "You will go and apologize to her, and you will behave yourself as long as she is in this house. She is your sister, and you will make it your business to get along with her."

"She's selfish and mean."

"No," said my father. "You're the one who's selfish and mean. You're only thinking of yourself, and you're jealous because her family's got more money than yours, and she's got a fancy bracelet and more bathrooms in her house than you've got in yours."

The tears rushed down my face. It was all so unfair . . . and maybe also a little bit true. I looked toward my mother. At least she should have been my ally in all this. Hadn't I stuck up for her? But she kept her eyes away from mine and repeated, "You just do what your father tells you."

"Go ahead now!" He gave me a little push, and I went. Slowly. But I went.

Beth was dressed, and combing her shiny, short hair when I came into the room. She stopped and waited.

"I'm sorry," I muttered.

She still didn't say anything, so I went on. "You're a guest in my house, my dad says, so I have to be nice to you."

Beth shrugged. "You don't have to be anything you don't want to be."

"Well, I don't want to be nasty, but you . . . you . . ."

She was looking me over, up and down and sideways. Her eyes focused on my face. "You've been crying," she said, with what sounded to me like pleasure.

"No," I protested, reaching up to wipe the leftover tears on my cheek. "It's hot. I'm sweating."

Now she was smiling. "You always were a crybaby," she said, "and you never were a very good liar."

"I'm not a crybaby," I said, forcing the tears back, "and I'm not a liar either."

"Oh, yes, you were," she insisted. Then she moved closer to me. "Do you remember anything?" she asked. "Anything about me?"

"I remember . . ." I began. But what did I remember about Beth? What was it?

We stood there silently, and then, suddenly, I remembered something else. "What was it you wanted to tell me?" I asked.

She shook her head. "What are you talking about?"

"Last night—in the middle of the night. You wanted to tell me something."

"Oh," she said, "yes, I did, but . . ."

"But what?"

"I don't know now," she said, with a weird smile on her face. "It isn't anything nice. Maybe you won't feel good if I tell you."

And I didn't want to hear it. I knew that. That weird smile on her face made me scared, very scared, and I wanted to stick my fingers in my ears and not listen. Whatever it was that Beth wanted to tell me, I didn't want to hear.

She stood there, watching me, waiting. I had to do something.

"What's your favorite color?" I asked her.

"What?"

"I know you don't like pink," I babbled. "So what color do you like?"

She moved back and shook her head. "What is it with you?" she asked. "What kind of dumb question is that?"

It wasn't going to work. I was scared, so scared that my knees began trembling. I sat down on the bed. "Please, Beth," I said. "I don't want to be nasty. Just don't be mean to her. I won't be nasty if you stop being mean to her."

"Who are you talking about?" She came and sat down next to me.

I didn't answer.

"Who?" she demanded.

"My mom," I told her.

CHAPTER 6

▼▼▼▼▼▼▼

"Listen, Molly," Beth said, "I want to tell you something that I guess you don't remember."

I didn't want to hear it. "Just don't be nasty to my mom, Beth," I said. "She's had a lot of disappointments in her life, and . . . please, Beth—"

"*She's* had disappointments?" Beth repeated, but not in the way I had said it. In a mean way. But I knew that if I kept on talking, she couldn't.

"Oh yes," I said quickly. "You know Alex had to marry Lisa because she was pregnant, and he had to drop out of school. My mom nearly freaked out about that. She was so proud of Alex, and now he's working as a computer repairman, and she's afraid he won't go back to school."

Beth shrugged her shoulders.

"And then there's Jeff."

Now Beth looked interested. "What about Jeff?"

"Well, he never even finished high school. He always thought he'd be a musician, and sing and play in a band."

"I remember. I remember," Beth said. "He used to have a bunch of kids over playing guitars, and there was one guy who played a trumpet."

"Right—and Mrs. Palagonia from upstairs kept complaining and complaining, and my mom tried to have them go and play somewhere else."

"I remember Mrs. Palagonia," Beth said, grinning now. Suddenly, I felt safe, and I grinned back at her. "Didn't she have twin boys—funny-looking twin boys?"

"Yes, she did. She does. But they're grown-up now, and they got to be real good-looking. You're right. They were funny-looking when they were kids."

"They had big noses?"

"Yes, they did."

"And zits?"

"Yes, yes. But now they're really good-looking. They're about Alex's age, and they still live at home."

"Oh, I wish I could see them. I wish I could see Mrs. Palagonia. I liked her a whole lot. And wasn't there a family with a baby downstairs? I think their name was something like Klondike?"

"Kronkite," I told her. "They moved three or four years ago."

"They had a beautiful baby girl. I remember that baby. Mrs. Kronkite let me hold her once on my lap, even though I was only four or five."

"She used to bite. The baby, I mean," I told Beth. "She used to bite, and her nose ran all the time. She turned into a real brat. I was glad they moved. But anyway, Jeff never finished high school, and he doesn't have a real job. He does get some gigs here and there, but nothing that really pays."

"He used to have a beautiful voice," Beth said. "I can't wait to see him."

"It's an okay voice, I guess, and he plays okay on the guitar, but nobody really think's he's that good. My mother wishes he would learn some kind of work to support himself. Every so often, my parents have to help him out. They keep saying it's the last time, but I don't think it ever will be."

"Girls!" My father was calling. "Come on. It's time for breakfast. We've got a lot to do."

Beth jumped up. "That's Uncle Walter. He's really great. I don't remember him as well as . . . as the others, but he's really nice."

"My dad? Oh sure, but Beth, so is my mom."

Beth just turned and walked out of the room.

We had a lot to do. Beth and I went shopping with my dad while my mom stayed home and pretended that she would relax over another cup of coffee and read the Sunday paper. I knew she would straighten up the house all over again, worry about the stains on the dining room tablecloth, suffer over the chips in the china, and set the table before we came back.

We had a long, long list, and we had to go to several stores. I was still shaky from this crazy fear. Why should I be afraid of something Beth wanted to tell me? What could it be? Whatever it was, I didn't want to hear it. I stayed quiet, but Dad and Beth chattered away as if they saw each other every day. Beth had opinions on lots of things.

"Don't you have a health food store around here?" she asked my father.

"I couldn't say," he answered, dropping a couple of heads of lettuce into the shopping cart.

"We always get our produce at the health food store," Beth told him. "We don't want to eat food that's been sprayed with poisons."

My father picked up a bunch of green onions. "I think our bodies learn to tolerate the sprays," he told her.

"I don't agree with you, Uncle Walter," she said. "I've done some research on the subject, and I think there's a strong correlation between food sprays and certain types of cancer."

"What about gasoline?" my father inquired, dropping three cucumbers into the basket.

"Gasoline is a major pollutant of the atmosphere," Beth stated.

"And does your family own a car?"

"Well, actually, we have two cars, but I don't approve."

"Do you go places with your parents in the cars?" My father began picking out tomatoes. "Maybe you both better give me a hand with these tomatoes. We're going to need a lot."

"Yes, I admit I do, but I'm not perfect." Beth grinned up at my dad, and he grinned back at her.

"No?" he said in mock surprise. "I thought you were. Okay, that's enough tomatoes. Why don't you go find two bunches of parsley, Beth? And Molly, you go see if they have any fresh basil."

We picked up bread, and we picked up a chocolate cake and some strawberries. We bought wine, even though nobody in my family drinks wine except for Jeff, and we bought some fresh flowers for the dining room table.

Back home, as I had expected, the house had been straightened up and the dining room table was set. There was a small tablecloth over the big one, which meant that Mom thought there were too many stains on the big one that couldn't be covered by dishes.

Mom was crying in the kitchen. Not because of anything either Beth or I had said, but because she was chopping onions.

"You'd better stay out of the kitchen," she said, her face wet with tears, as we carried in the packages. "Wait until I finish chopping the onions."

"Maybe I should bring the fan into the kitchen," my dad said. "It feels like a furnace in here."

"And I haven't even turned on the oven yet," my mother moaned. "But if you bring in the fan from the living room, then it will be murder in there later when the company comes."

"How about the little fan in your bedroom?" I said. "You could put that one in the kitchen and leave the big one in the living room."

My mother's eyes were streaming. "I forgot about that one. Mrs. Palagonia borrowed it three days ago when she had company, but she forgot to return it."

"I'll go get it," Beth cried. "I remember where she lives. Upstairs, right above you. In apartment 5C."

My mother just stood there with the tears running down her face and said nothing.

"I'll go too, Mom," I said. "She's home. Listen, you can hear her moving around. Or maybe it's Ted or Tom."

"I don't know. I don't know . . ." My mother hesitated.

"I think it's a good idea, girls," said my father. "Go get the fan back, if she doesn't need it. I'll unpack the groceries while you're gone."

Beth went flying down the hall, and I had to hurry after her to keep up. "Wait a minute! Wait for me!"

"Let's take the elevator," she said out in the hall. Her eyes were shining.

"For one floor? It would take more time to take the elevator than to go up the stairs."

"Oh, come on, Molly. I used to love that elevator. I remember I used to push all the buttons whenever we took it, and Mommy used to say I shouldn't."

"When did your mother tell you not to press the buttons?"

"I don't mean my mother, stupid. I mean . . . I mean Kathy."

She was pressing the Up button.

"Well, I'm not going to wait," I said, moving over to the stairs. "And I bet I'll get there ahead of you."

"Please, Molly." She put out her hand. "Come on—let's go together, like we used to."

"I don't remember ever going up in the elevator with you," I grumbled, but I stayed with her.

Inside, she pressed 5 and then, giggling, she pressed 6,7,8,9,10—all the way to the top.

"That's babyish," I said, but she didn't seem to hear.

She was still smiling when we stood in front of Mrs. Palagonia's door, 5C.

"Let me ring it," she said.

I shrugged my shoulders. Big deal.

She rang the doorbell, and her face looked the way a kid's face looks in the movies when she's opening a present with something wonderful in it. We heard footsteps, and she put her hands together in a kind of clap as the door opened.

It was Tom. "Hi, Molly," he said. "What's up?"

Tom was not as good-looking as Ted, but he was still very good-looking with his curly dark hair, his big blue eyes, and his very bright smile.

I could hear Beth take a deep breath, and when I turned to look at her, I saw that her mouth was open.

"This is my sister, Beth," I told him. "She's come for a visit."

"Nice to meet you, Beth," Tom said, smiling at her. Then he turned back to me. "Did you want to see my mother?"

"Uh-huh," I told him. "She borrowed a fan a few days ago, and my mom needs it back because we're having a lot of company, and . . ."

Tom opened the door all the way. "Come in. We're all going to visit my Uncle Joe out on the Island. It's a good thing you caught us before we left. Ma! Ma! Molly's here. She wants her fan back."

Mrs. Palagonia emerged from the living room. She hit her head with her hand. "I'm so dumb," she said. "Your mother was nice enough to lend me her fan, and I—" She stopped talking and looked at Beth.

"This is my sister, Beth, Mrs. Palagonia. She's come for a visit and—"

"Bethy," said Mrs. Palagonia. "This is Bethy, all grown up, little Bethy . . ." She held out her arms, and Beth immediately moved into them. "So wonderful to see you, darling," Mrs. Palagonia said, kissing her cheek. "I felt so bad . . . all these years . . . but, thank God, as your aunt says, it all worked out for the best."

Beth kissed Mrs. Palagonia too and said, "I remember the Christmas cookies you used to make. I remember they were big stars with shiny, silver balls, and once you made me a beautiful star all silver in the center."

"Oh, I haven't baked for years." Mrs. Palagonia laughed. "But it's true. You used to come and help me." She looked at me. "Molly was too little, but you used to come up. "Yes . . . I remember too. Come in. Come in. Sit down."

"Ma," Tom said, "we're supposed to be there by one. We don't have a lot of time."

"So we'll be late. This is such a treat for me to see Bethy. I can't tell you how I cried when . . . well, it's all over, and . . . come in, come in!"

We went into Mrs. Palagonia's cluttered living room with all the mirrors and pictures and little knickknacks. Beth looked around and smiled. "I remember the room just like this," she said, "with all your pretty things in it. And there was a little white china poodle with a gold collar. You let me hold it sometimes."

"Yes, yes." Mrs. Palagonia reached up on one of her crowded shelves of knickknacks and picked up a little china dog. "Here, sweetheart, here. You can hold it. You can keep it. I always wanted to give you a present, but there wasn't time."

Ted came into the room, car keys in hand. "Are we ready?"

"Teddy, this is Bethy. Do you remember Bethy, Molly's sister?"

Ted smiled and nodded. I don't think he remembered Beth just as Tom hadn't remembered.

"Mrs. Palagonia," I said, "my mom needs the fan back because the boys are coming over, and so is Beth's mother, and Lisa, and somebody named Ginger."

"Go, Teddy, get the fan. It's in the kitchen. And maybe you'd like to borrow the big one in the living room. You know, Bethy, I have air-conditioning in my bedroom. The boys are so good to me. And they want to put another one in the living room, but I don't know . . ."

"Ma," Tom said, "it's going to be crowded on the highway, and we're late already."

Mrs. Palagonia kissed Beth a few more times before we left with the two fans. She never kissed me like that, and she never gave me one of her little china figures either.

CHAPTER 7

▼▼▼▼▼▼

Beth pressed all the buttons in the elevator going down—4, 3, 2, 1. She giggled and looked around that hot, dirty little elevator as if it was Cinderella's magic coach.

I could smell the sauce cooking when I opened the door to our apartment. Beth was carrying the small fan in one hand and the little china dog in the other. I was carrying the big fan.

"Let's bring the little fan into the kitchen," I told Beth, putting down the big fan in the hall. "Later, we'll decide where to put the big one."

My mom and dad were both working in the kitchen. It was hot and steamy, but the smell of the cooking sauce made my mouth water.

"Look what Mrs. Palagonia gave me," Beth said, holding up the little china dog.

My father smiled. "You must really rate," he said. "She doesn't give anything away, and her boys complain that she keeps cluttering up the place with more and more junk."

"It's not junk," Beth protested. She looked down at the little dog and said, "It's beautiful. I remember how she used to let me hold it when I was little."

"No kidding!" my dad said. "I didn't realize you even knew her."

"Walter," said my mom, "Mrs. Palagonia's been living here longer than we have. She knew Kathy and Dan even before they had kids. She . . . she . . ."

"She's a very nice lady," Beth said, "and the boys are so good-looking." She began giggling. "They look like movie stars. I'm so glad I saw them. They were going to visit their Uncle Joe out on the Island. I think I remember him too. Isn't he a little fat man with a finger missing—and he used to play a game with us. He used to put his handkerchief over his fingers and make believe there was a bird underneath, and we . . ." She went jabbering on and on, waving the little dog around with one hand, and the little fan with the other.

My father reached over and patted Beth's head. "What a memory you have, Beth!" He turned to Mom. "It's really amazing what she remembers—things I've forgotten—good things. It's like time stood still for her while it moved along for the rest of us."

My mother's face crinkled up as if she were going to cry again, even though the smell of the onions had gone. I thought, she's hurting because she's remembering how Beth decided to go away with the Lattimores. It's making her feel bad again.

Beth stopped chattering. She looked over at the kitchen window, and her face collapsed into its usual tight, mean look. "I remember all sorts of bad things too," she said.

"Oh, sure," said my father. "Everybody remembers bad things." He shook his head. "It's easy to remember bad things, but it's nice the way you remember all sorts of good things too—like the game Mrs. Palagonia's brother used to play with you and her little knickknacks."

"I remember all sorts of bad things," Beth repeated, still looking at the kitchen window.

"Where do you want to put the fans?" I asked. "Mrs. Palagonia returned the little one, and she's lending us the big one from her living room."

"Oh, that's nice." My mom came alive. "Alex isn't bringing his because it isn't working right. Okay, so we'll put the little one up here on the refrigerator, and the big one—what do you think, Walter? How about in the dining room?"

"Makes sense," said my dad.

"Can I use the phone?" Beth asked. "I want to call my mother."

"Oh, that's right," said my mom. "She called. While you were upstairs. She said she'll be at the hotel for another hour or so, and you should call her back. I nearly forgot."

"Thanks a lot!" Beth's voice had a nasty sound to it.

My mom said apologetically, "I'm sorry, Beth, but I was so busy, it just slipped my mind."

"It's no big deal," I said, watching Beth's back as she moved down the hall toward the phone. I turned to my mom. "You don't have to apologize, Mom. She's just being a creep."

"Molly!" my father warned.

"Mrs. Palagonia fell all over her," I told them. "She acted like Beth was some kind of long-lost relative, and she kept kissing her and kissing her."

"Well, I guess it's been a long time," said my dad.

"And she gave her that stupid little dog to keep. She never gave me anything to keep, and she sees me all the time. Beth has all the luck. She . . . she . . ."

Both of my parents were standing still, very quiet. I stopped talking, and the only voice we could hear was Beth's, from down the hall. ". . . All grown up and so good-looking. And, Mom, she gave me a little china dog, Mom, a beautiful little . . ."

"I'm sorry," I said, looking up into my mother's worried face. I put my arms around her, and she bent over and whispered into my hair.

"It will be all right, Molly. Just a few more hours, and it will be all right."

"Okay," said my dad. "Let's get a move on. Come on, Molly. We'll set up the fan in the dining room, and Mom says we're all out of butter, so maybe you can run downstairs and pick some up."

"By myself," I pleaded. "Can I go by myself? Please?"

66

"Okay," my dad said. "I guess Beth will be on the phone for a while, if she's anything like you. I bet you'll be back before she's through."

"She's not anything like me," I told him.

Beth was off the phone when I came back with the butter. The kitchen was still hot and steamy, even with the fan going, and my mother's face, as she sliced the cheese, was wet with perspiration. She smiled when she saw me. "What's it like outside?" she asked.

"Miserable," I said. "Where's Beth?"

"In the living room with your father." She put the butter into the refrigerator, then turned to me. "Molly," she said, "be nice to her."

"I am nice to her," I said. "I try to be nice to her, but she's weird. Most of the time she's mean, but sometimes she's nice, and sometimes she acts like a baby. She was just crazy about the elevator. How can anybody be crazy about our dorky elevator?" I laughed, but my mother did not join in.

"Just be nice to her," she repeated. "In a few hours, it will all be over. She'll be gone, and . . . and everything will be back to normal again." She patted my cheek. "Maybe I'll take tomorrow off. I'm exhausted. Maybe you and I can have a day together. Maybe we can go to an air-conditioned movie and eat out."

"We can go to a movie," I said, "and maybe we can eat lunch out, but not dinner."

"Why not?"

"Because we'll have some of the lasagna left

over, won't we? We can eat it cold for dinner. Daddy likes it cold just the way I do."

"Whatever you like, sweetheart." Mom bent over the table again and resumed working on the cheese. "Only be nice to Beth."

I stood there, watching her. She looked tired and old and . . . something else. Something that frightened me and made me feel I had to do something to make that scared feeling stop.

"Mom," I cried. "Do you need any help, Mom?"

She looked startled. I guess I don't usually pitch in. She straightened up and smiled at me. "What a darling girl you are, Molly! But it's all right." She waved me off. "Go sit down and cool off near the fan in the living room. It really makes a difference with the two fans blowing toward each other. Maybe we should get another fan."

"Mrs. Palagonia says she has air-conditioning in the bedroom, and the boys want to put it in the living room too. She didn't tell me. She told Beth."

My mother lifted her apron and wiped her face. "This is the seventh day with temperatures in the 90's, and I think today is the worst. I wish to God it would break already."

I felt sorry for my mother standing there in the hot kitchen, and I didn't know what to do. I felt sorry for her, and for me and for—what? I felt scared and helpless, and I turned around and hurried away.

Beth and my father were both sitting near the fan in the living room. It did feel a lot cooler with the dining room door open and both fans blowing away at each other. My father was smoking and looking uncomfortable, and Beth was talking to him. ". . . Nearly a year and a half now, and he doesn't miss it anymore."

"Miss what?" I asked.

Beth turned and actually smiled at me. "Smoking," she said. "I was telling Uncle Walter how my father stopped smoking."

"Oh, Molly!" my father said happily. "Here you are. Tell us what it's like outside."

"Hot," I said. "Sticky, miserable, hot." I sat down. "It's not bad here with both fans on. Mom says we should buy another fan for the dining room."

"It never gets this hot in San Francisco," Beth said. "Anyway, Molly, I think you should get on Uncle Walter's case."

"What do you mean?"

"I mean you should help him give up smoking. I clipped lots and lots of articles for my father, showing the correlation of cancer to smoking. He didn't want to read them, and he kept telling me to stop it, but I didn't."

"I'm safe there," said my dad. "Molly never reads the paper, so I won't have to worry about that."

"You really should, Molly. You shouldn't let him keep smoking."

"Aw, Beth, I only smoke half a pack a day, except when I'm sitting around or when I'm with other smokers." He stubbed out his cigarette.

She kept talking to me, lecturing as if she was a

grown-up and I was some dumb little kid. She certainly could irritate people. "I mean it, Molly. If you love somebody, you shouldn't let him kill himself." She made a face. "And lung cancer is a terrible disease. You can't breathe."

"My mom keeps telling him to stop. The smoke makes her nauseous," I said.

Beth waved her hand impatiently. "I'm talking about *him*," she said. "You have to help *him* stop."

She smiled up at my dad. "Uncle Walter, do you know what finally convinced my father to stop?"

"You left him alone," said my father, trying to make a joke of it.

"No. I told him, 'Dad, I love you very much. And I want you to be around when I have kids. I want them to love you very much too.' "

The bell rang, and my dad leaped to his feet and rushed out of the room. Beth tossed her head, and her hair made a smooth, shiny wave across her cheek. "My dad used to run away from me too, Molly, but I didn't leave him alone until he stopped. You should really start clipping articles from the newspapers like I did. Now, here, in today's paper there's a wonderful article that . . ." She held out a part of the newspaper toward me.

"Do you want me to run away too?" I asked angrily. "Just get off my back, Beth. Just get off all of our backs."

Beth's eyebrows raised. "You're just ignorant," she said.

"And you think you know everything."

"I know a lot more than you do," she said. "I really can't believe we're related. You're such a . . . such a . . . birdbrain."

"And you're a pain," I said. "You make people feel bad. You made my dad feel bad, and you make my mom feel bad, and you try to make me feel bad."

"You don't know anything." Beth moved closer to me. I could see her eyes—brown, like mine, and her nose—kind of long, like mine, and her skin, dark, like mine. She had that weird, mean smile on her face again. "What goes on in that bird brain of yours? What do you think about besides eating and decorating your room in sick pink?"

"Lots of things," I said, moving back, and beginning to feel scared again.

"Like what?" She moved her face up closer. I could smell her breath, minty, like toothpaste. She was probably the kind of kid who brushed her teeth after every meal.

"I see my friends. I ride my bike. I swim. I . . ."

"Do you ever read a book? Uncle Walter says you never read a newspaper. How about books? Do you ever read books?"

"Sure I read books."

"Name one."

"I don't have to if I don't want to."

"Because you can't think of any. Because you can't think period."

I wanted to slam my fist into that mean, scary face of hers, but my mother's words, *Be nice to her,* and my father's words, *You will behave yourself as long as she is in this house,* froze me in my place.

"You're stupid," Beth said in the meanest voice I had ever heard. "You've had it easy all your life— just because you're little and cute. People always thought you were little and cute, and they always babied you and spoiled you. You've always been lucky. I remember . . ."

But I didn't want to hear what she remembered. I jumped to my feet and went tearing out of the room. If I had stayed there another second, I would have tried to kill her.

CHAPTER 8

▼▼▼▼▼

Aunt Helene was standing in the hallway, talking to my dad and mom when I escaped from the living room. They must have been talking about us because they stopped when I appeared, stood looking at me silently for a short second, and then Aunt Helene jerked back into speech.

"Oh, Molly, dear, there you are. How . . . how is everything going?"

"Oh, just great!" I lied, and looked at the boxes she was carrying in her arms. She had a bunch of them wrapped in different kinds of gift paper. It felt like Christmas. Christmas in August.

"Did you run into much traffic?" my father inquired politely.

"No, not bad at all," she answered and then handed my mother one of the boxes. "Karen, it's really wonderful of you to go to so much trouble for Beth and me."

"No trouble at all," said my mother, shaking her head over the box, a big square one wrapped in gold paper. I had a feeling it would turn out to be a box of candy. At least, I hoped it would. "And you didn't have to bring anything. You shouldn't have."

"Oh, just a few little things we picked up in Europe for Molly and the boys."

"You shouldn't have bothered," my mother insisted, and Aunt Helene said something about not bothering, and my father murmured something about trouble, and all the words began merging as I stood there, wondering which of the boxes were for me and what was inside them.

Beth appeared. I didn't turn, but I could see her mother look over my head and watch how her face grew happy. Imagine anybody feeling happy over Beth!

"Hi, darling," said her mom.

"Did Daddy call?" I heard Beth's voice behind me.

"Yes, he did, and he felt bad about missing you, so he decided he'd call again tomorrow morning."

Beth brushed past me and stood next to her mother. They were nearly the same height, but she laid her head down on her mother's shoulder for a quick second, and her mother, still holding the boxes, leaned over sideways and kissed the top of her head. "Are you having a good time, darling?" Aunt Helene asked. "I'm sure you are."

"Did you remember to bring Jeff's present?" Beth asked.

"Well, why don't we all go into the living

room," my mom said. "There's no reason for you to keep standing."

We all moved together into the living room, and Aunt Helene laid all the boxes down on the coffee table. Then she turned and smiled at me. "Now, I have a few things for you, Molly. I hope they fit. But . . ." She looked at me doubtfully. "You're built differently from Beth. She's taller."

"And I've got more of a figure," said Beth.

"Well, you're older, darling. A couple of years makes a big difference at this age."

I kept my eyes off Beth. I knew she had a bust and hips, and in my mind, I could see her undressed with a woman's body. Nothing much had happened to mine yet, and I wasn't sure I wanted anything to happen. But I didn't need to think about that today. I kept my mind on the gift boxes. There were six of them, all of different sizes. I hoped at least two of the big ones would be for me.

"You really shouldn't have," my mother was murmuring, still holding her own gold-wrapped box.

Aunt Helene selected a large, flat box, covered in dark green paper with a gold cord tie. It looked dull and it looked expensive. My mother was directing a tense, familiar look in my direction. I knew what she wanted me to do. "Thank you, Aunt Helene," I recited and heard my mother let out a breath.

I opened the box, unfolded the mysterious layers of tissue paper, and held up a plaid, pleated skirt with a big safety pin on the side.

"This is a real Scottish tartan," Aunt Helene explained. "I thought you'd like this one particularly—it's such a beautiful red color, and it's called Royal Stewart, the same one the British royal family uses."

"It's beautiful," I recited. "Thank you very much, Aunt Helene."

"Beth picked it out," Aunt Helene said. "She picked the same one out for herself, only in a larger size."

I hesitated and felt my mother's expectant look directed at me again. "Thank you, Beth," I muttered quickly.

"I got a size 12 for her," Aunt Helene was explaining to my mom. "I think it may be too large."

"Better that way," said my mother. "She'll grow into it. It's stunning, and I'm sure she'll love wearing it."

Right now, in all the heat, I felt sweaty just holding it, so I dropped it back into the box and covered it quickly with tissue paper.

Aunt Helene now held out another box toward me, a small narrow one. "Beth picked this out for you too, Molly."

"Thank you, Beth," I recited as I unwrapped it. There was a watch inside. It had a black leather strap, and on its face was a picture of a girl with long hair wearing an old-fashioned dress.

"It's lovely," I said. "Thank you very much."

"*Alice in Wonderland* was always one of Beth's favorite books," said Aunt Helene.

I smiled politely and wondered who the girl on the watch was.

"Whose picture is that on the watch?" my dad asked, leaning over my shoulder.

"Oh—well—it's Alice, Alice in Wonderland," Aunt Helene said quickly. "Of course, it doesn't really look anything like the Tenniel illustrations."

"I wouldn't know if it did." My father laughed uncomfortably.

"Go ahead and put it on, Molly," my mother urged.

I put it on, smiled, and said I liked it. But I thought it was dorky. I really preferred my digital watch, even though I usually forgot to wear it.

"And then, one for good measure—just a little something," Aunt Helene said quickly as my mother began to protest.

This box was in between the big one and the small one in size. I quickly unwrapped it and pulled out a pair of bright blue socks with lots of foreign words in bright colors.

"We bought them in Paris," said Aunt Helene. "All the words mean *I love you* in French. See— here it says *Je t'aime*, and here it says *Je t'adore*, and here it says *Mon petit chou*—that means 'my little cabbage.' "

"Did Beth pick them out?" I asked. The socks were cute, and I knew I'd wear them.

"Well, she and I did all our shopping together, so . . ."

"No," Beth said, "I didn't pick them out. I think they're stupid."

"Well, I like them," I said. "I think they're real cute."

"You would." Beth yawned and walked over to the window. She looked out and said, "That house used to be white. Now it's tan."

My dad laughed out loud. "Beth has some memory," he told Aunt Helene. "She's been reminding us of all sorts of things we'd forgotten. I think it's wonderful to have a memory like hers. She must be a great student."

"Yes, she is," Aunt Helene said. "Of course, it takes more than memory to be a good student. Beth works hard, and she reads a lot."

"I wish I could say the same for Molly," my dad said. "She never sits still for a minute."

"I do so, Dad," I protested.

"And I never see her reading."

"Well, Molly does just fine in school." Now it was my mom speaking. "And she has lots of friends. Everybody likes Molly."

"I guess that's true," my dad said.

Beth pointed out the window and said, "You know something else? There used to be a tree in that yard. It wasn't much of a tree, but I remember it had green leaves in the spring."

I picked up my boxes and muttered something about putting everything away in my room. I carried the gifts back and saw that my mother had straightened out my room. The trundle bed was back under my bed, which was covered again with my pretty pink spread. Everything was turning back to normal. I laid the boxes down on the bed. Tonight I would be sleeping in my own bed, and Beth would be gone. I couldn't wait.

"Molly!"

She was standing behind me.

"What?"

She came into the room and sat down on the bed. She shoved away the boxes. "I didn't really pick out that dumb skirt," she said. "My mom liked it. It was her idea for both of us to have the same one. And I didn't pick out the watch, even though I do like *Alice in Wonderland.*"

"I like the socks," I told her, "even though you didn't pick them out either."

We both smiled, carefully. I watched as she put up her arm to smooth her hair. The little charms in her bracelet tinkled. She tossed her head, and her beautiful hair rippled across her face. I could get my hair cut too, I thought. Maybe it would look like Beth's.

"I like your haircut," I said shyly. It was the first nice thing I had said to Beth since she arrived.

"My haircut?"

"It's beautiful."

"Well, you could get your hair cut the same way."

"Do you really think so?"

"Sure. You have the same kind of hair I do. It would look just the same."

"I don't know," I said. "I think your hair is prettier."

She tossed it again and smiled a big smile this time. She didn't look scary anymore. She looked just like other people. I sat down next to her. "Beth," I said.

"What?"

"Beth, how come you came back?"

"Because my shrink thought I should. He and my mother both thought I should."

"What's a shrink?"

"A psychiatrist. You know what a psychiatrist is, don't you?"

"Of course I do. It's a doctor who takes care of crazy people."

"You don't have to be crazy to go to a psychiatrist. You just have to have problems you need help solving."

"What kind of problems do you have?"

"Lots of them."

"Like what?"

She hesitated. Then she made a face. "Like you," she said. "You're a problem."

"Me?"

"Yes, you. I'm trying to work out my feelings about you. That's why we invited you out to California two years ago, and that's why I'm here now. Because my shrink feels it would be a good idea if I saw you again."

"Your shrink told you to see me and be mean to me?"

"I'm not mean to you."

"Oh, yes, you are—most of the time you are— and you're always mean to my mother."

"She's not your mother. She's your aunt. Don't you remember when you used to call her Aunt Karen? Don't you remember? You couldn't even say her name right, so you called her Aunt Kaka, and I remember—"

"Stop it!" I put my fingers in my ears but I could still hear her voice.

"Stop what?"

"Stop remembering."

She moved closer to me. "No, I won't stop. I'll keep on. And you know something? I bet you remember lots of things you say you don't remember, like right after the accident. I remember the two of them sitting there dead. And I remember my head hitting the windshield, and the screaming. I remember the screaming. It was you who was screaming. Nobody else. They were dead, and I was hurt, but you were doing all the screaming, even though you weren't hurt at all. I remember—"

I grabbed her, and the two of us rolled around and around on top of my bed, on top of the boxes. I got a hand in her hair, and she landed a sharp slap on my cheek. Neither of us yelled or screamed, and through it all we could hear the grown-ups talking and laughing from the living room.

It felt wonderful getting my hands on her. We thumped and slapped and bit each other silently and rolled off the bed onto the floor. She was bigger and heavier than I was, but I could move more easily and quicker. I rolled her over and jumped on her back and . . .

And then the bell rang.

CHAPTER 9

▼▼▼▼▼▼

"It's Jeff," Beth yelled, wiggling out from underneath me and leaping to her feet. She was panting,
her hair was messed, and there was a bite mark on
her chin. She went flying out of the room so fast, I
didn't have a chance to point it out to her.

I took my time. It didn't matter to me which
one of my brothers it was. I didn't care much for
Lisa, and if Ginger turned out to be like some of
Jeff's other weirdo friends, I didn't expect to like
her much either.

Finally, I pulled myself up off the floor and
looked in the mirror. My hair was all tangled up,
and there was a big, red splotch on one of my
cheeks. My shoulder ached as I picked up my hair-
brush and started brushing my hair. Next week,
for sure, I'd get it cut. Short.

I could hear the sounds of voices and laughter,

and I stopped to listen. Alex. It was Alex, not Jeff. Aunt Helene was saying something, and Alex was saying something, and my father's voice wove itself in and out. I brushed my hair and tied it back into a ponytail. Then I smiled at myself in the mirror. It had felt so good knocking Beth around. My fists clenched. Maybe I'd have another chance before she left.

I straightened my clothes and joined my family in the living room. Lisa was holding up some pink towels and smiling politely at Aunt Helene.

"Thank you, Mrs. Lattimore," she said, and Alex echoed it.

"Oh please—call me Helene," Aunt Helene said. "And now, here's a little something for the baby. Of course, we don't know whether it's going to be a boy or a girl, so . . ."

"It's going to be a boy," Lisa said. "I've had to have two sonograms because I'm having a terrible pregnancy."

I turned around and walked out of the room. Lisa just went on and on about all the problems she was having. I'd heard them lots of times, and I didn't need to hear them again. I moved into the kitchen, cooler now and wonderfully fragrant. The sauce was still cooking, and my mother had all of the other ingredients ready to be assembled.

I sat down at the kitchen table and looked up at the open window. Funny how Beth kept looking at that window. Why? I wondered. It was just an ordinary little window that looked out into somebody else's kitchen. What was special about that window?

Something tinkled from the living room. Our apartment was so small that you could generally hear most noises from one end to the other. Lisa must have finished talking about her pregnancy. I stood up and returned to the living room.

Lisa had unwrapped the other present—a little music box with a ballet dancer, standing up on one toe, and slowly revolving to a familiar melody.

"I really wanted some kind of lullaby, but this one was the prettiest," Aunt Helene said.

"Just darling," my mother said, "and you shouldn't have . . ."

"It's cute." Lisa examined it thoughtfully. "I guess it doesn't really matter if it's for a boy."

"Well, you could exchange it," Aunt Helene suggested. "I bought it this morning in a little shop near the hotel. There was a cute circus-music box, and I think a little baseball one."

"Really?" Lisa looked interested, but Alex said, "No. I really like this one. And, hey, I used to go to the ballet. Remember, Mom? I loved the *Nutcracker*, and a couple of times I took Molly."

Now he was smiling at me. I moved over to him and leaned against him.

"Well, we had a lot of names for a girl," Lisa said, still holding the music box, "but it's hard thinking of names for a boy. I like *Stuart.*"

"Yuk," I said, "that's a sissy name. The kids would call him Stew. Nobody wants to be called Stew."

"I like it," Lisa said. "My favorite uncle's name was Stuart, and everybody called him Spike. Anyway, I like *Stuart,* and Alex likes *Sam.* I hate *Sam.*"

"I hate *Sam* too," I said. "I hate *Sam* as much as I hate *Stuart.*"

"How about *Frederick?*" Beth suggested. "That's a nice name, and he could be *Freddy* for short. That's cute."

Lisa began wrapping up the music box, so I guessed she had decided to keep it. "Girls' names are easy," she said. "Both of us like *Amanda,* and we also like *Samantha.*"

"They'd call her Sam," I said. "That's terrible for a girl to be *Sam.*"

"Anyway," Aunt Helene smiled, "maybe you'll have a girl next time."

"I don't know if there will be a next time." Lisa leaned forward, eager to tell Aunt Helene all about what the doctor had said, and what she had said, and the nurse . . .

"So," my father said quickly, "what's new at work, Alex?"

Lisa stopped talking and began to smile. Usually, she doesn't like being interrupted while she's describing the symptoms of her pregnancy.

"Oh, everything's fine," Alex answered and then turned toward Beth. "It's wonderful to see you again, Beth," he said. "You and Molly look so much alike."

"Alex," Lisa said, still smiling, "go ahead and tell them."

"Later," Alex said.

"Tell us what?" My mother said suspiciously. She generally felt suspicious when Lisa looked happy.

"Go ahead, Alex, or I will."

"Well, it's no big deal."

"Alex!"

"Okay. Okay. They're making me assistant manager at the store. They want me to handle the retail end of it, and—"

"They're giving him a big raise," Lisa burst in.

"Well, it's going to mean a lot more responsibility," Alex said. "Of course, the money will be great."

"And school?" asked my mom.

"Well, I might not go back next semester," Alex said. "I will need to have a few evenings free, and . . ."

"And we'll have the baby," Lisa said. "I don't want to be home alone all the time with the baby."

"Maybe I can go back in the spring semester," Alex said.

"I'm going to go back myself in the spring," Lisa said. Lisa is a business administration major. "My mom said she'd watch the baby a couple of days a week for me."

"I'll watch the baby at night, after work," my mother said quickly, "so Alex can go back to school too."

"We'll have lots of time to talk about it, Mom," Alex said. "But now I want to hear all about what Beth's been doing."

"Lots of things," Beth said. "Mostly, I'm trying to figure out what I want to do with my life."

"Wow!" Alex said. "You're starting pretty early. I still haven't figured it out, and I'm nearly twenty-two."

"There's no hurry," Aunt Helene said, smiling

at Alex. "Sometimes it takes a lifetime, and maybe that's part of the fun of living."

"I don't know," said my mother, looking at Alex but not smiling. "Sometimes you don't want to wait too long."

The bell rang, and Beth jumped up. "It's Jeff," she cried. "That must be Jeff." She went flying out of the room, followed by my mother.

I raised my eyebrows and smirked at Alex. He smirked back. Nobody in our family ever gets excited over Jeff's comings and goings.

We stayed quiet, listening to the sounds of greetings and the chorus of voices. ". . . Murder outside . . . 100 at least . . . Ginger . . . my mom . . . Jeff . . . Jeff . . . Bethy, little Bethy, all grown up . . . watch the guitar . . . living room . . ."

Jeff came in first with his arm around Beth's shoulder. She was looking up at him as if he was Tom Cruise.

". . . Great surprise," Jeff was saying in his usual happy voice. Jeff always sounded happy. Even when my parents leaned on him, it was hard to stop him from being happy. ". . .Wonderful seeing you after all these years . . . you're just gorgeous . . . I can see the family resemblance . . . You don't look anything like Molly, though, but I think you look kind of like me. Doesn't she, Ma? . . . Oh, hi, everybody, hi . . ."

Behind him trailed Ginger, lugging a guitar. She was a heavy girl with dark hair. To my surprise, she was wearing a dress and high-heeled shoes. Jeff's friends, like Jeff, generally wore jeans, old, creased shirts, and running shoes. Ginger was smiling uncomfortably, like most people do when they come into a room full of strangers.

"Well, hi, Mrs. Lattimore," Jeff said, his arm still around Beth, moving across the room and shaking her hand. "It's just great seeing you again—and Bethy too. What a kick! Actually, I was thinking of coming out to California one of these days, just to see you all."

"I didn't know that," my mom said sharply.

"Any time," Aunt Helene said politely.

"Oh, Jeff, why don't you?" Beth cried. "We've got lots of room—you could stay for as long as you like. We've got a piano, and you and I could sing."

Jeff nodded and laughed. "Well, I just might. I have a couple of friends who've moved out to the Bay Area, and they say the scene out there is real mellow."

"This is Ginger," my mother said, with a hard look in Jeff's direction. "She's a friend of Jeff's. Ginger, this is my husband; my daughter, Molly; my son, Alex; my daughter-in-law—"

"Oh, don't throw all those names at her, Ma," Jeff said. "She won't remember them anyway."

"How do you do," Ginger said shyly.

She didn't have red hair, so I asked her, "Why do they call you Ginger if you don't have red hair?"

She looked helplessly over toward Jeff, who said, "Because she's got a real hot voice. I mean hot. When she sings, I have to warn you, people feel like they're going to burn up."

"I don't want to feel like I'm going to burn up," Lisa said. "I'm hot enough already."

"Oh, Jeff, can we sing like we used to?" Beth asked. "Do you remember how we used to sing?"

"Uh-huh." Jeff nodded. "It was great. Sure I remember." But I don't think he did.

"I'm thirsty," Lisa said. "Lately, I'm always thirsty. I'm not hungry so much anymore, but I'm always thirsty. The doctor says—"

"I wasn't thinking." My mother sprang up. "I have some soft drinks and"—looking toward Beth—"I made a big pitcher of lemonade. What would everybody like to drink?"

"I'll give you a hand, Mom," Alex said, beginning to get up.

"No, I'll help her," I said, pushing him back.

"Are you suffering from heatstroke or something?" Alex said to me.

"Ha, ha, ha!" I helped Mom carry in a tray of drinks and then followed her back into the kitchen.

"I guess I'll assemble the lasagna and put it up," Mom said.

"Why don't I give you a hand?" I offered.

"That's very sweet of you, darling, but wouldn't you rather be with the others?"

"No, I'd rather be with you, Mom. And to tell you the truth, I don't want to hear any more about Lisa's heartburn."

My mother smiled at me and reached out to touch my hair. "Your hair is so neat today. It really looks pretty."

"I like the way Beth's hair looks. It's so shiny, and I love the way it flips back and forth when she tosses her head. Next week, Mom, I want to get a haircut like that."

"I wish Jeff would get a haircut," Mom said. "And he needs a shave. He should have had a shave before he came. And why couldn't he put on a clean shirt? Why does he always have to look like such a mess?"

"Nobody else notices the way you do, Mom. He looks okay."

"That girl, Ginger," Mom said. "She seems like a nice girl. She thanked me for inviting her. At least she's got good manners, which is more than I can say for Jeff."

Beth came into the kitchen, smiling and carrying a couple of glasses. "Jeff wants more lemonade, and so does Ginger," she announced.

"I have more," said my mother, rushing off to the refrigerator. "I squeezed a whole bunch of lemons. There's plenty."

Again, Beth's eyes rested on the window while she waited for my mother to get the lemonade.

"Here, here," cried my mother, holding out a pitcher of lemonade toward Beth. It took Beth a moment or two to tear her eyes away from the window and focus them on my mother. The smile was gone, and her mouth was pulled tight over her teeth.

My mother poured some lemonade into each glass and then asked, "Do you want to bring the pitcher into the living room with you? Maybe somebody else wants some lemonade too." She looked happy and gave a little laugh. "I haven't made lemonade for ages. We always used to have it when we were kids."

But Beth just shook her head and walked out of

the room. My mother stood there, looking after her, holding the pitcher in her hand.

"Maybe I'll try some, Mom," I said.

I took a glass from the cupboard, and my mother poured some lemonade into it. "Yuk!" I said. "This is disgusting. I remember you used to mix frozen lemonade with grape juice sometimes. That wasn't so bad."

"We always used to make fresh lemonade in the summertime," my mother said, putting the pitcher back into the refrigerator. "Kathy always liked lemonade too. I remember now. She used to drink it all the time."

"Mom," I said, pouring the rest of the lemonade in my glass down the sink, "why does Beth keep looking at the kitchen window?"

"The kitchen window?"

"Uh-huh. There's something about that window that really fascinates her. What is it?"

"I don't know." My mother shook her head helplessly.

"She's funny," I said. "Sometimes she's so mean, and sometimes she's . . . well, she's like a little kid with Jeff and with Mrs. Palagonia. She really likes Daddy, and sometimes she's not bad with me. But, Mom, she's always mean to you. And you should be the one who's mean to her. She's the one who picked the Lattimores. I can't figure her out. And every time she looks at that window, she gets nasty."

My mother bent over the lasagna pans and began arranging the noodles. "You just be nice to her, Molly," she said.

CHAPTER 10

▼▼▼▼▼▼▼

By the time we put the pans of lasagna into the oven, Jeff had begun singing.

"Oh no!" My mother straightened up and listened. "He's not going to sing *that* song in front of them! Oh, no!"

"It's not *that* song, Mom. All of Jeff's songs sound alike, but this is a new one. I don't think we ever heard it before."

My brother Jeff composed songs as well as sang them. There was one that my mother particularly hated. It had to do with loving the whole world. She thought some of the lyrics were indecent, although he claimed it was all in her own mind.

"I'd better get in there," my mother said, whipping off her apron. "You never know what that boy's going to come up with."

I followed her back into the living room. Jeff was sitting in the center of the room, on the floor, with a plaid wool scarf wrapped around his neck. I guessed that was his present from Aunt Helene. My mother made an impatient sound that nobody else seemed to hear except me. Jeff was singing very loud.

> *No, no, baby, no, no, no!*
> *I say yes, don't let me go.*
> *No, no, baby, watch it grow.*
> *This love of mine just won't go slow.*

Ginger was plunking away at the guitar, and Beth was leaning forward, her mouth open, her eyes shining. The song seemed to go on longer than most of his songs. When it was over, Beth cried, "Oh, that was wonderful, Jeff, just wonderful."

"Very unusual song," Aunt Helene said. "Very—uh—the melody is certainly . . ."

"It's not really finished yet. I still think the lyrics need a little more work. But there's another one I wrote for Ginger." He looked up at Mom, standing in the doorway, watching him with a very concentrated look. All of us understood Mom's looks. Jeff laughed. "It's okay, Mom. This one is real pretty. I kind of stole the melody from Madonna, but the words are tame. Even you might like it. Come on, Ginger, let's do 'Beat, Beat, Beat.' "

"Well, sure, if it's all right with your Mom," Ginger said shyly, her cheeks very pink.

"I like the old songs," my mother interrupted quickly. "Why can't you sing some of the nice old songs?"

"I know lots of old songs," Ginger said. "Which old songs do you like? I know, 'I Wanna Hold Your Hand' and 'Saturday Night Was Meant for Fighting' and . . ."

"Well . . ." My mother was trying to think up a song that nobody would mind. You could see she was having trouble. "Well . . . well . . . I like . . . I know . . . I like a song like 'Ave Maria.' "

" 'Ave Maria!' " Jeff cried. "You've got to be kidding, Mom."

"I used to sing 'Ave Maria,' " Ginger said. "I was in my church choir, and we sang it every Christmas. I can sing it, Mrs. DeMateo, if you like."

"For God's sake, Ma, it's the middle of August. We're having a heat wave."

But Ginger began tuning up the guitar, and we all watched her. She strummed softly at first, and then sang in a low voice . . . "Ave, Maria . . . da, da, da, da, da, da, da, dum . . ." It was all in Greek or Latin, so I couldn't understand the words, but I could feel a ripple running all the way down from the back of my neck to behind my knees.

After a while, the strumming grew louder, and her voice opened up exactly the way Jeff had described it—into a big, strong, burning sound. The room felt too small and cramped all of a sudden.

"My God!" said my father when she finished.

"You have a wonderful voice, a splendid voice!" said Aunt Helene. "You could be a professional singer with a voice like that."

Ginger's cheeks shone bright red. "Thank you," she said in a little voice, looking down at the floor.

"You could sing opera with that kind of voice," Aunt Helene continued. "Do you take lessons?"

"No." Ginger continued looking at the floor. "I never took any lessons, but I always loved to sing."

I noticed Beth watching Jeff. He seemed surprised and maybe a little disappointed at all the attention Ginger was getting. I heard my mother make a few complimentary remarks, and even Lisa joined in. But Beth kept her eyes on Jeff.

"Jeff," she said finally, "could we sing together, the way we used to?"

"Sure, Bethy, sure." Jeff straightened up and took the guitar from Ginger. "What would you like to sing?"

"Don't you remember, Jeff? You wrote a song for me. Just for me, you said."

"No kidding!" Jeff grinned at her. "Just start us off, and I'll remember."

Beth began to sing. She had a high, sweet voice that didn't match the rest of her.

> *Let's hold hands and circle round.*
> *Some go up and some go down.*
> *But the prettiest girl in this whole town*
> *Is little Beth with eyes so brown.*

"You wrote that?" my mother said happily. "See, Jeff, if you just put your mind to it, you could really write some nice songs."

"And then, there was another one about two

mosquitoes, and one about a man with a wooden head."

"Just start it off for me, Beth."

Beth began singing, and after a while, Jeff joined in. They sang a couple of songs, and then Jeff laughed and said, "I forgot all about those."

"They're very nice," my mother said proudly. "Jeff, you really wrote some cute ones back then. Nice, catchy songs! Why can't you do the same kind now?"

"Oh, Mom!" Jeff said, but he began strumming, and soon some of the others joined in too. Aunt Helene was clapping, and Alex, who hardly ever sang, started to hum. Other voices blended in. Somebody laughed. I kept my eyes on Beth. She was laughing and singing. Her eyes were shining, and she didn't look mean at all. She looked the way she had looked upstairs in Mrs. Palagonia's apartment. There was no reason for it, but I began feeling scared again.

The smell of the lasagna began to fill the living room, and my dad put up his head, sniffed the air, and smiled at my mom. "I hope you made a lot," he said.

"Oh, that's right. I'd better get things moving," she said, turning around slowly and moving back to the kitchen.

"Wait, Mom!" I cried. I had to move. I had to be doing something to make that sick, scared feeling go away. "I'll help."

I followed her into the kitchen. She was stand-ing there, smiling. You could hear Jeff and Beth singing the loudest, and the other voices backing them up. "I guess it's all working out for the best," she said, "and isn't it wonderful how Jeff can behave when he isn't showing off?"

"Mom," I said, "he's not a kid anymore. He's twenty-four."

Ginger came into the room. "Can I help, Mrs. DeMateo?"

"No, no!" My mother smiled at her. "You just go back and enjoy yourself with the others."

"I'd rather help you," she said. "Can't I do something? Make garlic bread or a salad?"

"Well, that's very nice of you, but I don't want you to bother."

"I'd really like to. I work in a salad bar, I mean, during the day. Please let me help."

"I'll help Ginger," I offered. "We can both work on the salad."

"Well . . ."

My mother had always taught us the rule of three. According to my mother, if a person offers three times to do something, then that person is generally sincere. It also works if you're at a friend's house and her mother invites you to dinner. You should turn down the offer twice, but you can accept after the third time. Ginger had offered to help three times, which meant that she was sincere.

"If you two make a salad," said my mother, accepting Ginger's offer, "then I can cut the bread and finish setting the table."

It was fun working with Ginger, and my scared

feeling faded. I washed the vegetables, and Ginger dried them and cut them up into interesting shapes. She also answered my mother's questions. Yes, she had grown up in Queens. . . . No, she hadn't known Jeff very long . . . only a month or so . . . Yes, her parents were both alive, and she saw them a couple of times a week, at least. Yes, she had two other sisters but no brothers. . . . She used to think she wanted to be a cook, but now lots of people thought she should try singing. . . . No, her parents didn't like the idea, but Jeff had encouraged her, and that meant a lot to her.

I could see that my mother approved of Ginger. The salad grew as Ginger and I added cucumbers, onion rings, radishes, carrot swirls, celery, and let-tuce. From the living room, the sounds grew louder and louder. Suddenly my mother stopped washing off the serving pieces to listen.

"It's Walter," she said, giggling. "I haven't heard him sing since . . . since . . ."

Buffalo Gal, won't you come out tonight
and dance by the light of the moon?

my dad sang.

"Will you just listen to that man!" My mother's face was flushed.

"He's got a nice voice, Mrs. DeMateo," Ginger said.

"Well, yes, he does," my mother agreed, wiping her hands on the towel and hurrying out of the room. "That's where Jeff gets it from."

Ginger put both hands into the big salad bowl and tossed all the vegetables. "She's nice, your mom," she said. "I was afraid she wouldn't like me."

"Oh, she likes you, all right," I told her. "You can always tell when she doesn't like somebody."

"Your dad's nice too," she went on, "and so are the rest of you. You've got a real nice family."

"Well," I told her, "Beth and her mom—they're not really our family. I mean, Beth is my sister, but her mother really isn't my aunt."

Ginger stopped tossing and looked at me in confusion. "How can Beth be your sister and her mother not be your aunt? As a matter of fact, if Beth is your sister, shouldn't her mother be your mother?"

"Never mind," I said. "It's too complicated. Anyway, what kind of salad dressing do you think we should use? We have French, Italian, and, I think, a low-cal one." I opened the refrigerator and held up a few bottles of salad dressing.

"I can make a dressing," Ginger said. "If you have oil and lemon and garlic. But getting back to Beth and her mother . . ."

"I'll explain it all to you later. Anyway, we've got lots of lemons. We have nutmeg too, if you need it."

"No," she said and then smiled. "But if you have ginger, I could make a really good salad dressing."

The sounds from the living room grew louder. "That must be Lisa singing," I said, making a face. "I never heard her sing before."

"Jeff can really get a whole group going," Ginger said. "He's such a great person."

"I guess you like him a lot." I handed her a bottle of olive oil and a lemon. "I'll go see if I can find any ginger."

"Everybody likes Jeff." Ginger's cheeks grew pink again.

My mother came back into the kitchen, her cheeks as pink as Ginger's. She was smiling and shaking her head. "Your father!" she said to me. "Sometimes he forgets his age."

Jeff was strumming very loud on the guitar now, and my father was bellowing away some old song about not stepping on his blue suede shoes.

"Anyway, I think it's time to take the lasagna out of the oven before it gets too dry."

"It smells wonderful, Mrs. DeMateo," Ginger said, pouring the oil into a bowl. "I'm starving. I didn't eat any breakfast."

My mother opened the oven, picked up some pot holders, and pulled out two pans of lasagna. She set them both down on the stove, and Ginger and I moved over to look at them.

"Oh! Oh! They're beautiful!" Ginger said.

"I don't know." My mother was trying not to sound too proud. "I probably could have used some more basil, and I'm not sure the sauce isn't too thin."

Suddenly, as if the message had gone out that the lasagna was finished, the music from the living room stopped, and our small kitchen filled with starving people.

"Oh, my!" Aunt Helene was standing behind me. "Will you just look at those lasagnas."

"Nobody," said my father, "nobody makes lasagna like my Karen." He put an arm on her shoulder.

"I'm dying of hunger," Jeff moaned.

"All right!" My mother was now the boss. "Everybody go into the dining room and sit down. Anywhere you like. I'll bring in the lasagna, and we'll cut it at the table. Ginger, toss the salad. Molly, here, take in the bread. Walter, see if there are enough chairs around the table."

"Is there any more lemonade?" Lisa asked.

"Yes, there is," I heard Beth say. "Should I bring in the lemonade, Aunt Karen?"

"Yes, darling, yes," my mother said, her face bright with happiness. "You bring in the lemonade."

CHAPTER II

▼▼▼▼▼▼▼

At first the only sounds were the clatter of dishes passing back and forth, and the voices blending: "Is there more sauce? . . . Lisa, do you have enough? . . . Please pass the salad . . . not enough forks . . . butter . . . another piece of bread . . ."

And then there was the eating and the sounds of forks on plates and satisfied voices sighing over my mother's lasagna. How it happened that her lasagna was so perfect, and everything else she cooked so ordinary, I'm not sure. She said she learned it from her mother-in-law, my father's mother, who was my grandmother but not Beth's grandmother. Anyway, my dad said that his mother never even made lasagna, and that my mom must have learned it from somebody else.

It was hot in the dining room in spite of the

two fans blowing at each other. I noticed Aunt Helene's face glistening with perspiration. She dabbed at it with her napkin, but it didn't stop her or any of the rest of us from eating our lasagna. She ate hers slowly and neatly, while I gobbled mine down and was the first to finish. I knew I had to wait for somebody else to finish also before I could ask for seconds. I'm not a big eater generally, but I can never get enough of my mom's lasagna. Sometimes I just keep on eating and then, suddenly, I'm sick.

So I sat there, waiting and watching the others eating. Aunt Helene was the slowest. She took tiny pieces on her fork and chewed them the longest. My dad, for such a big man, also took small pieces and chewed slowly, never taking his eyes off the plate. Lisa talked more than the others, saying how she had pretty much lost her appetite and describing some of the symptoms of her heartburn in between gobbling her food.

My mother ate the least. She was busy passing things back and forth, urging this one to have some grated cheese, asking that one if he or she wanted bread. She nodded at me, as I sat over my empty plate. It pleased her to see that I hadn't forgotten my manners and wasn't asking for seconds until some of the others had finished their firsts. My mother looked happy. I saw her eyes settle on Beth as she ate her lasagna and drank her lemonade.

Ginger was sitting across the table from me and next to Beth. There was still a little lasagna on her plate, but she caught my eye, leaned forward, and said, "I think I finally figured it out."

"What?" I asked.

"I finally figured out how Beth can be your sister and her mother not be related to you."

She was speaking in a low voice, but Beth heard her and turned to listen. She was putting the last piece of lasagna from her plate into her mouth.

"It must be that you're really half-sisters. You have different mothers, but the same father." She looked up the table to where my father sat.

"No," I said, "it's more complicated than that."

"It's not complicated at all." Beth finished chewing her lasagna and laid her fork down on her plate. "Our birth parents were killed in an accident, and Molly was adopted by our aunt and uncle. Aunt Karen is my birth mother's older sister. She decided to adopt Molly, and I was adopted by my mother and father. So that's why my mother isn't actually Molly's aunt, although her mother is my aunt and her aunt too."

"But I like to think of myself as Molly's aunt," said Aunt Helene. There still was some lasagna on her plate, and she picked up another dainty piece on her fork.

"Oh!" said Ginger.

"Do you want some more lasagna, Molly?" my mother inquired. Lisa had finished and was sending her plate down for seconds.

I didn't feel as if Beth had explained our history accurately. I particularly didn't like the way she said my mother "decided" to adopt me. So I added,

"Beth *decided* to go with her parents. She didn't want to stay with us." Then I passed my plate down, and my mother lifted a piece of lasagna from the pan and held it poised over my plate.

"That's not true," Beth said in a loud voice.

"What's not true?" My mother slid the piece of lasagna onto my plate. "And do you want some more lasagna, Beth?"

"No!" Beth pushed her plate away. "I don't want any more lasagna. And it's not true that I wanted to go with my mom and dad then. It's not true. She only wanted Molly. That's what's true."

My plate with the second helping of lasagna remained in front of my mother.

"That's a lot of baloney," I cried, leaning toward her. "You picked Aunt Helene and Uncle John. You didn't want to stay with us."

"Molly!" I heard my father's voice.

"Beth, dear," said her mother, "we're all having such a nice time. Why don't we just—"

"I want to get it straight, once and for all." Beth stood up and looked straight at my mother. "Isn't it true, Aunt Karen, you didn't want me? You sent me away. Isn't that the truth?"

"I'm sorry." Ginger put a hand on Beth's arm. "I didn't mean to make any trouble."

I jumped up too. "Go ahead, Mom," I yelled. "Tell her the truth. Tell her how bad you felt when she picked the Lattimores."

My mother stood over the second pan of lasagna, holding a spatula. She shook her head. "No," she said. "No, it isn't true."

"What isn't true?" Beth demanded.

My father said gently, "It isn't true that we didn't want you, Beth. Of course we wanted you, just as we wanted Molly. But as Karen always says, I'm sure it all worked out for the best. And now, maybe it's time for seconds all around."

"No!" Beth's voice was shrill. "She didn't want me. She sent me away. I came home from the hospital with both my arms in casts and hurting all over, but I remember, I was happy. I mean, I wasn't happy because I was hurt or my parents were killed, but I was happy because I was coming back home. That's what I thought. I thought this place would be home."

"Well, it could have been home for you—" I began.

But she interrupted me. "Shut up, Molly! Shut up! You don't remember. You don't remember anything."

Her voice had grown shriller, and her mother stood up and moved over toward her.

"I came home, and nobody else was here except her. She brought me home, and she took me into the kitchen, and she gave me some lemonade. I sat there drinking it at the kitchen table, and I was happy to be home. I was looking at the curtains— I loved those curtains—when she said . . . she said . . ." Beth broke into loud sobs, and her mother put an arm around her shoulder but didn't try to stop her from talking.

Beth gulped the air and then continued. "She said I was going to stay with a wonderful woman who would take care of me until I was better. I said I wanted to stay here with her and Molly and the boys, but she said she had to work and couldn't take care of me. She said this wonderful woman had a wonderful family, and she would take good care of me until I was better. She said this woman was used to taking care of sick children, and she and Molly would come lots of times to see me until I was better. She said . . ." Beth was shaking now, and her tears and sweat ran together, making her face wet and shiny.

"She said I would have fun there. I looked at the curtains, and I drank my lemonade, and I believed her. She always made lemonade then. My . . . my birth mother used to make it too, and I always loved it. But I didn't have fun, and the woman wasn't wonderful. I hated her—her name was Mrs. Morgan, and she kept me in a room by myself, and if I cried she . . . she . . ." Beth's voice blurred, but I could hear what she said. "She shut the door."

"No! No!" My dad said, very clearly. "I remember you were in kind of a convalescent home. Wasn't that what it was, Karen?"

"It was a foster home," Beth shouted. "And whenever she came—and she brought Molly only once. But I guess you don't remember that, do you?"

She turned her wet, shiny face toward me, and I looked away and said, "No, I don't remember."

"No, of course you don't remember. You don't remember anything." Now her voice was lower and meaner. "But *she* came a few more times after that. And she kept telling me it would all work out for the best. Even then she told me that. And I cried, and she didn't listen. I begged her to take me home, and after a while, she stopped coming. Then Mrs. Morgan told me I was going to stay there. She said I should just make up my mind and stop bellyaching. That's what she said. I remember what she said. And then, one day—it was a miracle—my mother—only she wasn't my mother then—she came to see me. And I told her. And she could see how they were treating me. She could see I was abused and neglected."

"Well," Aunt Helene said, her arm tightly around Beth's shoulder, "you weren't really abused, darling. Mrs. Morgan had two other children, and she was very busy. I'm sure she meant well, but—"

"She put me in a room and shut the door."

"I know, darling, I know." Her mother smoothed her hair and kissed her cheek. "You weren't happy there, and we—Daddy and I—we wanted you so much." She looked at Ginger. "We couldn't have any children, and we were hoping to adopt one. So when Beth was brought to the hospital—I had her in my ward for several weeks—I guess I just loved her from the start. We weren't even sure she was going to make it, and she was such a wonderful, enchanting child, I used to tell my husband about her, and he started coming in to read to her."

"Such silly books." Beth was suddenly laughing and crying at the same time. "He tried to read me *Moby Dick* and *A Tale of Two Cities.*"

108

Her mother was laughing too. "Well, he didn't know anything about children, but he learned, didn't he, darling? Anyway, we didn't know at first that Beth—that we could adopt Beth, but I just had to see her again after she left the hospital. And I found out where she was and visited her, and—"

"And you saw that she didn't want me."

"Karen!" Uncle Walter stood up. "I think you need to make it very plain to Beth and to everybody else that she is under some kind of misunderstanding. She was in a convalescent home, as I remember, and once she recovered we were ready and eager to have her come home. Weren't we?"

My mother shook her head and sat down.

"Karen!" my father insisted. "Beth has made a very unpleasant accusation against us, and—"

"Not you, Uncle Walter," Beth said. "I don't remember anything bad about you. Only her. She was the one."

"I'm sure you're mistaken. I know how I always felt, and I'm sure we—"

"We," repeated my mother, looking at him. "We."

"Of course," said my father. "We would have taken Beth, just as we did Molly."

"There was no *we* then," said my mother angrily. "Then there was only me."

"Yes," Beth cried. "There was only you."

"Yes," my mother agreed, standing up again. "There was only me. And I had two young boys to look after and . . . and an alcoholic husband."

My father sat down and looked at his plate.

"I'm sorry, Walter," my mother said, very, very slowly. "It was a long time ago, and you worked it out finally. You're a good man now, and you're a good father now, but then I was all alone, and I couldn't . . . I couldn't take any more. I couldn't save the whole world."

"It wasn't the whole world," Beth cried. "It was only me. And I loved you. And I thought you loved me. I thought . . ."

My mother sat down and started to cry. She put her face in her hands, and her shoulders shook.

"I didn't mean anything," Ginger said. "I'm sorry. I never should have asked."

"It's better you did," Beth said. "I needed to tell her, to have it out with her. She can't deny she sent me away. She can't deny it."

My mother wasn't denying anything. She kept on crying, and the rest of us just sat there, listening. My mind was flashing with sounds of screams and crying, and I felt so frightened, I couldn't move.

Finally Lisa said, "You have to stop being angry, Beth. It seems to me like you've got wonderful parents who love you."

"Yes," Beth said, "I do. And I love them."

"So it worked out okay then. My mother-in-law is a very good woman. She's had to put up with a lot in her life, and it hasn't been easy for her. Everybody makes mistakes, but as my Uncle Stuart used to say, 'You have to forgive and forget.'"

"I can forgive," Beth said, "but I can't forget."

"Better to forget." Jeff was talking now. "Lots of things you have to forget to stay normal."

"Like what do you have to forget?" Alex asked. "Your problem seems to be you can never remember."

But Jeff was looking at my father, and Alex followed his eyes and suddenly grew silent. My father continued to sit still, looking down at his empty plate. An alcoholic? My father? No, I couldn't remember him drinking anything more than Diet Coke or coffee. But my father sat there, stooped over his plate, saying nothing, and my mother's face was still buried in her hands.

The scared feeling inside me moved up to the top of my head and down into my toes. There wasn't any part of me that wasn't scared. I looked at Beth's red, angry face, and I hated her so much, I thought I would burst.

So many secrets that weren't mine. So many terrible memories that I was shut out of—that I couldn't remember, memories that were cruel and that hurt people I loved. I was helpless against all those memories.

It all happened so quickly. I was scared and helpless, and in my head, the screaming began again and went on and on. I put up my hands to my head to make it stop, and inside of it, inside the screaming, I remembered.

"You had a doll," I cried, pointing my finger at Beth, "a baby doll with a pink dress and a bonnet, and she said it was your doll, not mine."

"What? . . . What did you say?" Beth turned to look at me, astonished.

My mother lifted her face out of her hands.

"Mommy said it was your doll, and I should

play with my own, and I cried because I wanted yours so bad."

"Now, Molly, you stop that!" Alex said sharply. "You don't always have to be the center of attention."

"No." Beth wrinkled up her face. "No, I never had a doll with a pink dress. I had a Barbie doll that *she* (looking at my mom) gave me once, but I never—"

"Yes, yes, you did." Now I was crying the way I had then, when I remembered how I had wanted that doll. "And Mommy was mad at me, and I kept crying—it was in the car. Before it happened. And then . . . then you let me have it. You said I should stop crying, and you'd let me play with it. You . . . you"—I was crying very hard now—"You were nice to me then."

"I don't remember," Beth said. "I don't remember a baby doll with a pink dress. Are you sure?"

Now I was the one who had to gulp the air in order to continue. "She had such a beautiful face, that doll. But then it happened—and she wasn't beautiful anymore. Her head broke in pieces in my hands, and I screamed and screamed—"

"I don't remember," Beth said. "I just don't remember."

It was very quiet in the room, and then Jeff began laughing. My father straightened up and looked at him.

"What a wild day!" Jeff said. "This is turning into a real encounter session. Maybe there's somebody else who wants to unload some fascinating memory that nobody else remembers. No time like the present."

"Jeff!" my father rumbled.

"Sorry, Dad, but, hey, if nobody else wants to come up with an interesting memory, I've got a few I wouldn't mind sharing with the rest of you."

My mother was directing one of her concentrated looks at him, and he turned toward her, smiling. "Just kidding, Mom. You know I was just kidding."

Alex laughed, and Lisa drank some water, and Beth sat down. Aunt Helene hesitated and then returned to her own seat. But nobody wanted any more lasagna, not even me.

CHAPTER 12

▼▼▼▼▼

"You're not really like what I'd thought you'd be," Beth told me.

We were in the kitchen, and she was getting ready to leave. The grown-ups were out in the hall, talking. I braced myself.

"I mean I thought you were going to be very pretty, and—I don't mean to insult you, Molly, but you do look a lot like me, I guess, and I'm not exactly a raving beauty."

I thought I was prettier than she, except for her hair, maybe, but I kept it to myself.

"And I thought you'd be more of a spoiled brat."

Look who's talking, I thought, but I kept that to myself too.

"But you're not really mean or selfish, I guess, even if you are undeveloped. Of course you're still young."

She put up her hand to smooth her hair, and the charms on her bracelet danced.

"That is such a beautiful bracelet," I told her. "Did you get it for a birthday present?"

"What? This?" She looked down at it. "No, it used to be my mom's. She liked charm bracelets when she was a girl. Actually, I have three others. Do you want it?"

"What?"

She took it off and held it out to me. "Here. It will be something to remember me by."

"Oh, Beth, I don't know. It looks so expensive."

"Go ahead, take it, Molly. I've got three others."

So I took it and slipped it on my wrist. It was so beautiful, I wanted to throw my arms around somebody and kiss her.

But not Beth. I still felt shy and awkward with her. "Thank you, Beth," I said. "But now you have to take something from me. What have I got that you'd like?"

She was looking at the kitchen window again, and I knew what it was she wanted.

"My earrings," I said. "I got them for my birthday, and I want you to have them. They're beautiful, and I want to give you something special."

She took them and said thank you. But I knew I couldn't give her, nobody could, what she really wanted.

I sat on my mother's lap after everybody had gone home. We were in the living room—both my parents and I. My dad was smoking a cigarette and sitting in the chair in front of the fan. My mother and I were on the couch. I could hear both of the fans whirring and the sounds of car horns rising up from the street.

"Mom," I began, "if I had been the one who was hurt and away in the hospital. If it had been me—"

"No!" My mother tightened her arms around me.

"But, Mom, you said you couldn't take any more. You said you couldn't save the world. You said you were alone . . ."

My father stubbed out his cigarette and lit another one.

"Now, Molly, I want you to understand one thing. Your father is a good man, a wonderful man, and I wasn't blaming him."

"It's all right, Karen, you can blame me. You should blame me. It's a long time ago—maybe it isn't such a long time—eight years ago—but Molly, I drank, and your mother—she threw me out then. The boys remember. They don't like to talk about it, but they remember."

"He was always good to them, Molly," my mom said. "I mean he never hurt them but—"

"But I went off on binges, and I spent money, and I kept getting fired from my jobs."

"So that's why I wasn't myself when the accident happened. I was deep in my own troubles. And your father—well, he came out of it soon after, and he's been a real rock ever since."

"But, Mom . . ." I needed to ask her the one question that still plagued me.

"I think maybe it's a good thing Beth spoke up,"

said my father. "Maybe we all need to be re-minded of things that happened. Maybe if we re-member, we won't make the same mistakes again."

"She was wrong," my mother said. "I didn't send her away—not forever. But I couldn't take care of her then. I just couldn't."

"If I'd been on my feet, you could have," my fa-ther insisted. "So don't go blaming yourself. I'm the one you should blame. I'm the one Beth should blame. You had too much responsibility for one person."

"I needed time," my mother said. "I would have taken her, once she recovered but . . . but . . . then the Lattimores got into it, and everything changed. I would have taken her, but then I was half out of my mind. I was close to cracking up myself. And Mrs. Lattimore kept pressuring me. She was dying to take Beth, and by that time, Beth . . . well, Beth wanted to go with them."

"Mom!" I tried again. "Mom, if it had been me who was hurt, would you have put me into that foster home?"

My mother's arms rocked me back and forth. She didn't answer my question, but I knew what the answer was.

We sat comfortably, quietly, for a little while, listening to the sounds of the fans and the cars below. It was still very hot, and I could feel the heat in my mother's arms spreading into my own body.

"The most terrible thing," my mother said fi-nally, "is Beth . . . what I've done to Beth. She hates me so much. She'll always hate me. There's nothing I can do and nothing I can say. But I was in terrible shape then—and I know I would have taken her, once I got back on my feet again. I know I would have. I just needed time, and if Mrs. Lattimore hadn't pushed and pushed . . ."

"I think Beth understands now," my dad said. "She's no dope, and I don't think she ever realized what you were up against. Okay, she got it off her chest, and she heard what you had to say, and I'm sure she feels better now."

"Do you really think so?" My mother looked anxiously at him. "Do you think she . . . she's not so angry at me anymore?"

"I'm sure she isn't."

I held up my wrist. "Look, Mom, she gave me her charm bracelet, and before she left, she said she was glad she came."

My mother let out a breath and nodded. I didn't tell my mother what I think Beth will always know and what I think all of us know. Nobody said it out loud, not even Beth exactly. But Beth knows and I know that my mother/my aunt could choose only one of us then, and she chose me. Why? It wasn't because I hadn't been hurt. It was something else, something more important, something wonderful for me and terrible for Beth. How could she ever forgive my mother or forgive me for being the one she picked? I was glad that Beth's family loved her the way they did, and I knew I would never, ever be jealous of her again.

My father suddenly laughed out loud. Both of us

turned toward him, startled. "That Lisa!" he said. "Did you hear what she said?"

"Can you ever *not* hear what she says?" my mother said impatiently.

"No, no, Karen. I think you missed what she said about *you.* You were out of it then, but she stuck up for you when Beth was carrying on."

"I never heard that," said my mother.

"Oh, yes," I chimed in. "She said something like 'My mother-in-law is a real good woman,' and that it's been hard for you, and that Beth had to forgive and forget."

"She said *that?* Lisa?"

"Uh-huh, and she told Beth that she was lucky to have parents who loved her and that she had to stop being angry."

"Are you sure Lisa said all that?"

"Oh yes. Then, later, she started talking about her heartburn again."

My mother smiled. "Well, I guess maybe even she has a few good points. I tell you what, though. I really liked Ginger. She's about the first friend of Jeff's I've ever liked."

"She's crazy about him," I said.

"Jeff?" My mother rolled her eyes up to the ceiling. "Well, I must say she's a nice, polite girl. And her clothes were very neat. Maybe she'll have a good influence on him."

"What a voice!" said my father. "She can really blast you out of your seat with a voice like that."

"And I was surprised at those cute songs Jeff was singing with Beth. He really can come up with some nice songs—some nice, clean songs—if he tries."

"He's going to California for Christmas," I told my parents. "Aunt Helene invited him and Ginger, and they said yes. They invited me too."

"Well, that's okay." My father lit another cigarette.

My mother didn't say anything.

"I don't think I'll go."

"You can go if you want to," said my mom. "She's a nice person, I guess, Mrs. Lattimore, and Beth . . . well . . . Beth is your sister."

"She doesn't feel like my sister," I said. I didn't say that we both feel awkward when we're together or that Beth really doesn't like me. It's not a good feeling knowing somebody doesn't like you, even if you know why. I would like to see her house, though, and check out those bathrooms. But not for a while. "Besides, I'd rather stay home. We had a lot of fun last year."

"Jeff won't be here," my mother said. "I hope he doesn't stay too long with the Lattimores. Sometimes that boy doesn't have any sense at all."

"We'll have Alex and Lisa—and the new little guy," said my dad.

"I hope they don't call him Stuart," I said. "That's a terrible name for a boy." I leaned back against my mother, and I felt such a rush of happiness that I had to close my eyes to keep it all inside of me.

"You know something?" my father said. "It's crazy, but I'm actually hungry."

"Me too." I opened my eyes. "And we've got lots of lasagna left and salad and French bread."

My father waved impatiently. "I don't want any bread or salad—but a little piece of that lasagna—cold lasagna . . . How about you, Karen?"

"No, I'm not hungry. But I am thirsty."

"They drank up all the lemonade," I said. "But there's 7-up and Diet Coke."

"Funny how she remembered that I used to make lemonade." My mother smoothed my hair. "Kathy used to love it, too, the way Beth does, but you"—she smiled at me—"you always hated it, and the boys didn't care one way or the other. I guess I stopped making it after Kathy died, and Beth . . . Beth went away. I forgot how I used to make it all the time."

"She's a good kid, basically, that Beth," said my father. "She's smart and talented, and I have to hand it to her how she's interested in the world. She'll make something of herself, you can be sure of that. But the things she remembers make her angry. And she has some memory. Maybe it's not so good having such a memory."

"She forgot about the baby doll with the pink dress," I said.

"I hope she'll begin to forget other things too," said my mother, easing me off her lap.

"What are you doing?" I complained.

"I'm going to get some food for you and Daddy."

"I'll help," said my father, beginning to rise.

"No, Walter. I think I'd like a few minutes by

121

myself." My mother walked out of the room, and my father and I looked at each other.

"She's still upset," my father whispered.

"I know."

"It's too bad." My father shook his head and took a deep puff at his cigarette. "She's a wonderful woman, your mother, and I gave her a terrible time of it."

"It's all over, Daddy," I said, moving over to him. "You heard what Lisa said. We have to forgive and forget."

I sat down on his lap and rested my head against his chest. I knew he was feeling bad, and I loved him so much, I wanted to do something to make him feel better. The smell of his cigarette was caught up by the fan and circulated around me. "Daddy," I said, "you have to stop smoking or you'll get cancer. It was in the newspaper today, Beth said." The paper was lying, neatly folded, over on the ledge in front of the window. I jumped off his lap, picked it up, and began leafing through it. "I'll find it for you, Daddy. I want you to live a long, long time. I want my children—"

"Molly!" My father's face was twisted up in horror. "Molly, you're sounding just like Beth. Don't tell me you're going to turn out like her."

I giggled and continued sifting through the paper. I knew I wasn't going to turn out like Beth. I didn't know who or what I was going to turn out like, but I knew I was happy and I knew I wasn't afraid.

Temple Israel
Minneapolis, Minnesota

IN HONOR OF THE BAR MITZVAH OF
MICHAEL S. FELDBAUM
FROM
THE FELDBAUM FAMILY

MAY 7, 1994